Raff

The Vorge Crew – Book Four

By Laurann Dohner

Raff by Laurann Dohner

Lilly left Earth seeking adventure, and learning about aliens sounded cool. She just didn't expect to meet any in person — until her ship is attacked by alien pirates. Now she's meeting plenty of them. Scary ones who want to do very bad things to her.

Fighting for survival since childhood, Raff Vellar is more intimately familiar with knives and bloodshed than women. Then, during a trip to his home planet, a tiny human literally falls at his feet. When he learns she's been forced into slavery, a fierce need to protect the human overcomes him. A feeling that quickly turns into a deep need to keep her forever.

The Vorge Crew Series List

Cathian

Dovis

York

Raff

Raff by Laurann Dohner

Copyright © November 2018

Editor: Kelli Collins

Cover Art: Dar Albert

ISBN: 978-1-944526-99-3

Chapter One   **6**

Chapter Two   **19**

Chapter Three   **35**

Chapter Four   **48**

Chapter Five   **57**

Chapter Six   **74**

Chapter Seven   **95**

Chapter Eight   **109**

Chapter Nine   **118**

Chapter Ten   **128**

Raff – The Vorge Crew – Book Four

By Laurann Dohner

Chapter One

Raff hated Gluttren Four. Few good memories had been made while growing up on the planet. It was a hellish place. The majority of the residents lived in three locations. Those cities were built on large plateaus. They were high enough not to be washed away by the seasonal flooding the surface endured and the wildlife couldn't climb the steep inclines to the top. Many deadly beasts called G4 home.

Few dared to live in the outlands. If the floods and animals didn't kill someone in the lower altitudes, the banished convicts from the cities could. They were known to mostly murder their victims for the clothing, weapons, and food they could take. Sometimes they'd keep their victims alive, enslaving them.

Raff had mostly lived in a city growing up but he'd also spent a few years in the outlands. He'd missed Yessepiti beast meat. The first thing he'd done was hunt one down in the outlands and cook it over an open fire. It was his favorite meal. He'd waited until the worst of the heat faded, evening approached, before he'd flown to Daba City. It used to be his main home.

He entered the huge crashed ship that had been turned into the biggest trade market on the planet. It didn't take him long to track down Mannel. The big ugly alien was scarred over every inch of his hardened shelled skin and now missed one of his three eyes. He was known for trading information at a price. Raff walked up to the male who stood a few inches shorter than him to glare.

"Shit. What are you doing back, Raff?"

Raff just continued to glare at him but he tapped his thigh, his fingers close to the razor-sharp blades mounted there. Mannel glanced down, turned an ugly shade of purple, and inched back.

"Tell me what you want to know. I have contacts. Please don't kill me. Anything you want is yours."

"I always ask you the same thing. Where's Eldet?" That was the same enemy he tracked every time he entered the solar system.

"Dead."

Raff tapped his thigh.

"Really. Not a lie this time. He surfaced from hiding four months ago after weeks of rain. Prix caught him. His body is still hanging near the auction area as a warning to all. Go look."

Raff considered that. Weeks of rain would cause the lower levels on the planet to flood. Most of the caves out there would completely fill, making them unlivable. All the supplies Eldet could have stored would have been either ruined, sunk where he couldn't reach them, and it would have forced him to return to the city to resupply.

He spun away and stormed through the market. The residents kept a wide berth of him. He ignored their scared looks. Most recognized him and those who didn't were wary of his looks.

Raff had always stood out on Gluttren Four. Few alien races were as tall as him and even those weren't as thickly muscled. None of them had his predatory facial features either. It had made him a target as a kid until he'd taught them to never mess with him. That had meant he'd had to maim or kill a lot of adult bullies.

He came to where some of the residents sold their goods and stared up at the bodies hanging from the ceiling rafters far above. There were dozens of them. He finally spotted the one he sought, approaching it from below. Each corpse had been dipped in sealing oil to keep them from rotting and there was no doubt that was Eldet. His throat had been slit. Disappointment hit. Raff had wanted to be the one to kill the cowardly bastard.

"You're back. Should I be worried?"

He turned as the heavy footsteps approached, recognizing the voice. He stared into Prix's eyes. They had once been friends as children and needed each other into adulthood to survive. At least that's what the term friendship passed for on the planet. A person could only trust someone else as long as they had a reason to keep them around and breathing. That wasn't the case anymore between the two of them. Raff had left without a backward glance when his cousin and *The Vorge* crew had come looking for him on the miserable planet. It had pissed Prix off to lose his ally.

The male stopped eight feet back, at least four guards with him. Prix now basically ruled that part of the planet, according to rumors. He confirmed them when he spoke. "You have no reason to return to my city, Raff."

"You knew I would return for Eldet. I wasn't going to let that go."

Prix grinned but it didn't reach his cold, dull eyes. "Still holding a grudge. I see some things never change. I was around when he popped up again instead of you. That male was always one to cause trouble. I had my own issues with him." His expression hardened. "Are you here to stay or just passing through?"

"I'll be going now." Raff pointed up to the body. "That was my last reason to ever step foot on this shithole."

One of the guards, a young kid Raff didn't know, snarled low. "Who are you to insult our home?"

Prix threw out his arm and hit the kid hard in the chest, knocking him on his ass. "Silence. Raff was born here and could kill you easy." He never took his attention off Raff. "This one still has a lot to learn. I don't want a problem with you. It's rarely worth the effort."

"No problem." Raff noticed a lot of motion toward the stage where they showed off merchandise to sell. A group of Raxis aliens carried in boxes and crates from one of the shops, setting them up.

Prix followed his gaze. "I get a percentage from all sales and my choice to take what I want. It's a profitable alliance. They needed a base of operations."

"If you don't mind giving disreputable pirates safe harbor. I wouldn't trust or turn my back on a Raxis. They are known for slicing the throats of their allies." It disgusted Raff. Then again, not much happened on the planet that was legal or right. "I'm leaving."

"You can take Eldet's body if you want it. For old times' sake."

Raff curled his lip and scowled. "Not necessary."

"You're seriously leaving for good?"

Raff nodded. "No reason to return. That's the last one." He'd already killed the six other men who'd murdered his mother. He didn't know how to feel about that. It had been his goal since he'd lost her. The seven males had come after him that day. Only he hadn't been at home. Just his mother. He'd had to hunt some of them across the surface into caves where they'd fled. Only Eldet had evaded him every time he'd been able to visit G4.

Prix met his gaze. "I'll walk you to your shuttle."

Raff didn't blame Prix for wanting to personally escort him to make sure he left. His 'old friend' would be worried that he'd take over if he planned to stay. "I'm not lying."

"I have nothing better to do."

"Fine. Walk with me." Raff turned, making his way through the crowded market. Selling tables were set up on both sides of the wide space. People moved out of their way, giving them a wide berth again.

There was suddenly yelling in front of them and Raff watched as a few people went down, as if they were being pushed. He froze, his hands gripping the handles of his blades strapped to his thighs, prepared to fight.

Prix growled next to him and reached for his own weapons. "What is going on?"

Raff assumed that meant Prix wasn't sending a team to attack him when his old friend stood at his side, facing the threat with him. A small body covered in a torn robe shot out of the crowd and came right in their direction. He saw her face since she didn't wear a hood. It was a female with four male Raxis pirates hot on her ass in pursuit. They were the ones shoving bodies out of the way.

It stunned Raff to realize she was a human. He could identify them easily now by their delicate facial features and small ears with lots of hair on their heads. There were three women from Earth on *The Vorge*.

One of the alien males who chased the female grabbed her by her long black hair. She screamed, turned, and he saw a flash of metal in her fisted hand. It was a knife.

The male reared back, letting her go, and blood ran down his fingers from a wound on the back of his wrist where she'd stabbed him to break free. Another Raxis made a grab for her. She kicked out in the oversized garment she wore that hid most of her body and flashed some of her pale skinned leg.

Her bare foot slammed into the alien's groin. The male screamed and landed on his ass, cradling his crotch. The female turned, running again. A third Raxis raised a stunner weapon and shot her in the back.

She made it a few running steps before she fell, landing damn near at Raff's feet. He stared down at her. Her hair had tiny blue streaks running through the long black mass. It was long, curly and wild. The Raxis who'd shot her stomped forward to retrieve the unconscious female but paused when he spotted Prix.

"Overseer Prix." The Raxis holstered the weapon. "Apologies. This slave is the new one you purchased. Feisty and untrained. I didn't think these things could fight. She'll be punished severely for escaping from

11

your brothel. We were preparing her for her first customer when she acted up."

Prix growled. "She won't bring in a good price if you mark her up with a whip or your fists."

Raff stared down at the female on the ground. "When did you start peddling slave flesh for sex profits?"

Prix turned. "I opened two brothels since you left. Good earnings."

That news sickened Raff. There used to be only one brothel on the shipwreck. An older female had owned and operated it. All the women who'd worked there had done so willingly. They had the ability to say no to customers they didn't want to touch for whatever reason. He'd been turned down plenty of times by some of them because of his reputation. He never would have harmed the females but they didn't know that. Guards had been there to protect them from violence. The poor human at his feet was a different story. She'd been bought and sold.

Prix was a cold-hearted bastard for forcing women into that line of work. Raff highly doubted the females were given any choices or protection. He kept his tone cool to hide his disgust and tried to use logic to protest her abuse. "This one looks fragile. I can't see her lasting more than a few customers. What's the point? It doesn't sound too profitable."

Prix snorted. "Slaves from other worlds bring in top dollar. Something new and she's only one species. That makes for excellent breeding stock. I don't sterilize these ones, hoping they get pregnant and birth more daughters I can earn money from. I'm not a fool. There are rules to follow for customers who pick fragile females. To kill one would mean to pay a steep price to replace my merchandise."

The woman began to stir at Raff's feet and a soft moan came from her.

The Raxis looked at Prix. "She needs punished and trained, sir. No one is going to rent her when she tries to bite and kick them. She turned wild when we were attempting to strip her and hasn't stopped fighting since."

"That tiny thing?" Prix suddenly bent and grabbed the female, hauling her up by her neck.

Raff tensed when he got a good look at her face now that she remained still. Her delicate features were striking for a human. At least he thought so. It might have helped that her dark hair was such a contrast to her pale skin.

She had big light blue eyes, which also surprised him. They were a color he'd never seen before. Her features were attractive too, despite a bruise marring her skin on one check and her bottom lip bleeding, probably from slamming into the ground. The stunner weapon had left her body weak and Prix shook her trying to get her to stand on her own feet. She managed to do it but swayed a little.

"You listen to me, whore," Prix hissed. "No more fighting or you'll be beaten. Then you'll lose me profit."

The woman blinked a few times, seeming to come out of her daze. "I'm not a whore."

"You are whatever I say you are, whore." Prix gave her another shake and glared at the Raxis. "Get this whore cleaned and stun her again if she doesn't listen. I doubt the client will care if she's awake when he climbs on top of her."

Raff could imagine the kind of hellish short life she'd face if he didn't do something. Gluttren Four residents were tough, growing up in the harsh conditions of the planet. A fragile human wouldn't survive the men who'd pay to use her body, especially if a dozen assholes rented her every day to abuse for an hour at a time. He thought of his crew and their humans. They'd want him to buy the human to save her.

The human suddenly clawed at Prix's hand still holding her by her throat. Her nails were enough to tear his skin, drawing blood. He roared in rage and threw her on the ground. She landed on her ass hard.

Raff moved fast when he saw Prix reach for one of his blades, knowing he'd kill the female just to prove no one hurt him and got away with it. Raff pulled his own blades out and put his spread legs over the female's lower body to protect her.

"No."

"Move, Raff," Prix yelled. "I'm going to gut that whore and string her body on the rafters to show what happens to stupid females."

"Don't kill the human. I'll buy her from you."

Prix still looked killing mad. "She disrespected me. It's my right to gut her. I want to hear her screams and watch her die. She's not for sale."

Raff tensed, ready to take on the Raxis, Prix, and his four guards. He didn't dare glance away from the threat but he needed to tell the human what to do.

"Human, get up and stay behind me. I won't let them kill you."

She hesitated but then one of her small hands curled around his calf and he almost expected her to hit him. She didn't. Instead she used his leg to help her get to her knees and she stood, pressing against his back. She wasn't a tall female. He could feel that. He also noticed that she reached for one of his daggers, yanking it free.

"I'm your only shot at survival," he warned low, knowing she could hear him. "Use that on me and they'll put your dead body on display as an example to others. Look up."

"Oh shit," she muttered, her voice sounding her horror.

"What are you doing, Raff?"

He glared at Prix. "Sell her to me. Otherwise, we're going to fight. I don't want trouble but you know I never back down from it."

"You're outnumbered."

"It wouldn't be the first time," Raff reminded him. "I'm still breathing. Can't say the same about them. You killed the murderer I wanted. Sell the female to me for old times' sake. I'm leaving and never returning to Gluttren Four. That should make you feel generous."

Prix glanced around. The market had gone quiet, the crowd watching. Raff could guess his thoughts.

"For old times' sake," Raff repeated louder. "We go back to childhood. Do me this favor, old friend. Make a profit off her. Sell her to me. I'm leaving and never returning. It means you won't see her again either."

Prix glared at him.

Raff reached down and slid out a marts bar. It was a lot to buy a slave. "It's all I've got on me." He lowered his voice. "I'm willing to kill to take her. How much have you spent on training your men? How many are you willing to lose? The cost difference isn't worth it."

"Are you getting soft since you left our world, Raff? Starting trouble with me over a whore? That's unlike you."

He gave Prix a cold smile. "Whatever you want to call it. I like human females. I'm keeping this one."

Prix seemed to consider it. "No. Get out of the way or die. You have ten seconds to comply."

He lowered his voice. "Human? Drop to the ground into a tight ball and stay put. Look at the ceiling again. That's where your dead body will end up if you don't do what I say."

He felt her drop between his legs. She kept his dagger though, not returning it to his belt she'd pulled it from. She went to her hands and knees and hunched down. He adjusted his boots closer to her waist to pin her body between his legs.

Prix backed up and lifted his hand, making a gesture with it. Two of Prix's guards rushed forward to attack.

Raff sucked in a deep breath and threw his blades, hitting the approaching males in the throats. They staggered back, clutching at the blades buried deep, before falling over. He went for his daggers lining his belt next, twisted his upper body, hoping the human followed directions by holding still and not moving. She'd trip him, if he didn't outright step on her.

He threw his daggers in rapid succession, taking out the four Raxis by targeting their throats too. It was the fastest way to kill. They fell back, blood spraying. He whirled around, bent, and grabbed the small guns hidden inside his boots.

Screams of panic erupted from the marketplace. Shoppers and merchants ran to leave the area or to seek a place to hide. It helped him know who to kill. His enemies ran at him instead of away. He opened fire on the last two approaching guards as he straightened before they could slam into him.

Prix tried to flee and dove toward a nearby table. His body cleared it and he fell out of sight. The jackass knocked it over to give himself cover. Raff spun, avoiding stepping on the huddled human at his feet, and shot more advancing guards. He saw Prix's head lift out of the corner of his eye and dropped one of his weapons, reached for the back of his neck, and yanked out the longer blade he kept sheathed down his spine. His finger and thumb pressed the two points on the handle to activate it. He threw it at table and watched it stick deep into the wood.

He twisted, crouched, and put his body over the human. A loud blast deafened him as the bomb inside the handle exploded. He waited to see the destruction until after the pieces of the table flew through the air and landed around him. It stopped and he turned his head.

Prix was down, not moving, and covered in blood from where the blast had thrown him. It was tempting to go make certain he was dead but there wasn't any time to spare. More guards would be scrambling to their location after hearing a bomb go off.

Raff rose, grabbing hold of the human's arm as he did, to pull her up to her feet. "Grab the back of my belt and don't let go. We need to move.

Stick close. We're not out of danger yet. I have a shuttle waiting nearby. We need to get the hell off the surface fast."

She didn't speak but grabbed hold of the back of his belt. He took off, mourning the loss of so many weapons he didn't have the time to retrieve, making her run to keep up with his longer strides. Weapons were replaceable though. Life wasn't.

His gaze darted around, looking for any signs of another attack. Most of the aliens they passed avoided his gaze or stayed on the ground where they'd dropped. He made it out of the market ship and crossed the desert strip to where shuttles were parked.

He was glad to see no one had messed with his ship. The force field protecting it glowed blue to show it hadn't been tampered with. The tiny shuttle wasn't much but he owned it.

Chapter Two

Raff made it to the shuttle and punched in the code on his wrist bracelet to drop the shield. The door slid open when it sensed him and he reached back, grabbed the human by her wrist, and yanked her roughly in front of him to put her back to his front.

"Don't fight me if you want to live. They are going to come after us hard and fast. Do everything I say."

She looked up at him, fear showing in her eyes. He hated the sight but didn't have time to explain more. He wrapped his arm around her waist, lifted her higher, and threw them both inside the cramped cockpit of his shuttle. His ass hit the only seat and her rounded bottom slammed onto his lap. He released her, reached up to hit the engine switch with one hand, closing the door with the other.

The loud sound of the engines coming on line was welcome and he grabbed the human, grateful she wasn't big, and adjusted her on his lap to give him access to the controls in front of him. Her body felt stiff, her breathing ragged from their running, but she wasn't fighting him or screaming. He was grateful for that. They needed to lift off fast.

Something hit the side of the shuttle with a loud ping. He flinched, grabbed the thruster control, and shoved his knee against the dash to brace since he didn't have time to buckle in.

"Hold on!"

He pushed the thrusters full blast and the shuttle lifted straight up, violently. That caused the woman to make a whimpering sound. The force of the maneuver at least kept them in place as they rapidly shot into the sky. He needed to get out of weapons firing range before they took out his engines or thrusters. He watched their elevation and finally eased off when they reached eight thousand feet. An alarm chirped at him and he snarled, his gaze going to the screen to his left to glance at the readout.

"Fuck! We have a breach in the hull."

The human on his lap looked at him, seeming paler than she had before. The blood on her lip looked stark in comparison. He hated to see terror in her eyes and figured letting her know what was going on might calm her a bit and make the situation less frightening. Talking much wasn't his thing but he'd try more for her sake.

"We can't break atmosphere with a breach. We're stuck on the planet for now. I won't let them get you."

He had to adjust her body to reach the comms. A display of light out of the corner of his eye and another alarm went off. It signaled that they'd been targeted for missile fire. He turned his head, staring down out the side window, and saw what appeared to be a flare shooting toward them.

Prix must have upgraded the city's defenses. He reached around the human and grabbed the controls, flying them the hell out of there. The missile tried to follow but it disengaged after a few miles and the attack alarm silenced. The hull breach one still beeped. They couldn't leave the planet but it didn't mean they had to hover above the city to remain targets.

Once he flew them three hundred miles away he had the craft hover in place again, Raff reached for the comms. They weren't damaged at least. He opened a channel to *The Vorge*, hoping they were still in range.

He'd told them he'd be on the planet for a week, not less than a full day. His crewmates had dropped him off early in the morning to go visit a station located on the other side of the solar system.

"Dovis?" He waited.

The male responded within seconds. "What's wrong? I didn't expect to hear from you for a week."

"I had problems."

"Are you injured? If not, we'll pick you up when planned. We've already set a course and are fourteen hours out."

Raff grit his teeth. He knew the male purposely tried to piss him off just to see how many words he'd get out of him. Talking wasn't Raff's thing. "I rescued a human from slavers and had to fight my way out of Daba City. They got a lucky shot and pierced the shuttle hull. Bounty hunters will be sent after us if Prix survived. Come get us and send down the larger shuttle."

"Shit. Prix is that bastard who tried to kill us when we first came looking for you, isn't he? The prick that didn't want to let you go because you were his main muscle? Are either of you hurt? I'm changing course."

Raff glanced down at the human on his lap. "That's Prix. Female, are you hurt more than the damage to your face?"

"They shot me with something."

He sniffed. "I'm only smelling a faint scent of blood but your lip is busted. Where is the other wound?"

She lifted her arm and shoved up the robe covering her skin.

He saw a tiny bloody scratch on the meaty part just under inner elbow. "The shot barely nicked you. You got lucky. They missed."

Her lips turned down at the edges of her mouth and then she licked them with a little pink tongue. "A shot as in a syringe. They injected me with a drug. That's why I started fighting so hard. They said it would make me livelier, whatever the hell that means. I feel lightheaded and weird."

Raff tried to think of what they'd inject the female with. He reached up and gently gripped her jaw, forcing her to turn her head more his way. She tensed but didn't struggle as he leaned in closer, staring deeply into her light blue eyes. They were a pretty color but alien. He couldn't tell if anything was wrong with her by studying them.

"Weird how? Can you be more specific? Do you feel sick, as if you will lose the contents of your stomach? Do you feel as if you're going to pass out?"

She blinked a few times. "Drunk. Really drunk and thinking is hard to do."

"We're coming," Dovis spoke, reminding him comms were still open. "I'm increasing speed to make it back there in twelve hours. I take it you got away for the moment?"

"We did," Raff confirmed. He was concerned about the female, trying to guess what Prix would have ordered the woman drugged with. He'd have to get the med kit to run a scan on her.

His shuttle blared another alarm and he cursed when he realized why. Two shuttles were inbound. He adjusted the female on his lap again and grabbed the controls. "I'm going to have to hide us, Dovis. Remember the cave where I picked up my belongings from? That's where I'll be."

22

"As if we could forget. We didn't have a shuttle small enough to land there and had to climb down with rope."

Raff remembered Dovis bitching at the time and thinking the male had been afraid of heights. "Hurry. We're out." He cut comms. "Hang on, female. We need to lose our pursuers."

He dove the shuttle toward the ground to take them off radar. The human gasped and grabbed hold of the sides of the seat. He didn't have time to belt them in and doubted the straps would fit over the bulk of two bodies anyway. He leveled his shuttle out about twenty feet from the ground. It left him dodging large rocks and the occasional tree. He found one of the deep gorges and drove down into it.

"We're going to die," the female softly whimpered.

He inhaled, smelling the sweet scent of her fear. "We won't. I know this planet well. I have a hidden cave that no one else knows about." He hoped it hadn't been found, at least. "My crew is coming for us soon. I'm not going to allow you to be recaptured."

It was cute how the female turned her head and pressed her cheek against his chest. He dared to glance away from where he piloted for a split second. She'd closed her eyes to avoid seeing how close they were to the canyon walls and outcroppings they flew under. His shuttle was small and cramped but he'd bought it for its ease with maneuverability. It also would fit inside the cave.

Fifteen minutes later he slowed his speed and narrowed his eyes, searching for the outcropping that marked his hidden lair. He spotted it and dove down, nearly hitting the canyon floor. They didn't but another alarm blared to let him know of an impending impact. He slowed his

23

speed to a hover, turned the shuttle, and activated the camera in the back to carefully reverse thrusters. He had to fly upward a bit to reach the cave entrance forty feet from the ground. He eased them down on the rock surface and shut off the engines.

The female still had her eyes closed. He'd have thought she might have passed out but her hands gripped the edge of the seat tightly still.

"We're here."

"I feel sick. It was all that weaving back and forth you did."

He activated the door to open and cool, fresh air blew inside. "Out," he ordered, not wanting her to throw up all over him and his control console. He gripped her hips with both hands and lifted her off his lap to help her up. She didn't weigh much.

She managed to get to her feet and stumbled outside. He wanted to follow but he took the time to search for the hull breach. It was located on the left side in the storage compartment. It was just a small hole but that was enough to kill them if they attempted to reach *The Vorge* in space. He climbed out, grabbed the med kit from behind the seat, and then exited the shuttle.

He also removed the imager shield and walked to the cave entrance, programed it, and let it go. The device flew out of the opening and seconds later, it erected a protective barrier. He would have missed the slight flash if he hadn't been watching for it.

"What is that?"

He turned, staring at the female. "Protection in case they followed us. They'll see sheer rock instead of the opening. It also will feel like rock if anything touches it from the other side. The shield won't allow anything to enter after us."

She stared out the opening. "But it looks like nothing is there."

"We can see out but nothing can see in."

She bit her lip but then backed away from him. The female had come to a halt near the fire pit he'd built as a youth. It was a round circle of rocks. A camping mat remained on the floor next to it. Behind that area lay a pool that was only about five feet wide that ran the length of the back of the cave. Memories instantly filled his head of the years he and his mother had spent there when they needed a place to hide. He didn't have time to dwell on the past.

"Take a seat, female. I have a med kit. The mat probably isn't clean but it's more comfortable than the floor will be."

He glanced around, glad to see the recent flooding hadn't reached his cave. There were large cracks in the canyon floor near it, making for great runoff when the rains came. It was part of the reason his mother had picked it. A fresh water source and a natural drain made for optimal survival in the outlands.

She turned, gaining his attention. "I'm fine."

"You are not. You said you felt sick." He crouched, setting down the kit, and opened it. "You also stated you've been drugged. I have a scanner that can tell us what you've been dosed with. I had the medical android update it for me to include humans."

She didn't take a seat. He withdrew the scanner and rose. More fear showed in her eyes and her body tensed. She even raised her arms. It was cute. She seemed prepared to fight him.

He resisted smiling. "I didn't rescue you to only hurt you myself. There's no need for you to punch me with your tiny fists." He showed her the scanner. "It will draw blood to test. It's harmless. Please take a seat."

She still hesitated, annoying him.

"I swear I won't hurt you, female."

"Lilly," she whispered. "That's my name."

It was a nice sounding one to his ears. He needed her to trust him. The blood on her lip bothered him and he worried about any injuries he couldn't see. Her robe covered most of her body.

"I'm Raff. You have my word that you are safe now, Lilly. My cousin is life-locked to a human from Earth. I'm aware that you must have been through quite a lot but I just wish to help you."

"Life-locked? What is that?"

He remembered the term Nara used. "Married."

That shocked the little human enough for her mouth to open and she sucked in a sharp breath. He saw suspicion narrow her eyes and could guess what she had to be thinking.

He found it cute too. "By choice. Nara willingly married my cousin. They are in love. She demanded he keep her. It's why I had human medical information added to the scanner on my shuttle. In case Nara was ever hurt. She's family to me."

Lilly was afraid to trust anyone. The big alien she faced off against was huge and appeared super strong. He also looked as if he were the adult result of an old Earth's version of a Viking warrior having a baby with

26

a lioness. He stood tall, had huge muscles, and had an actual mane of blond hair. His eyes were all lion but he almost had the facial features and body of a large human. There were also some sharp looking fangs she'd seen peeking from between his lips when he'd spoken to her. His body was covered in skin though, instead of fur.

His golden colored exotic eyes were beautiful, but he was some predator cat species of alien. He looked deadly and she'd watched him kill at least a dozen men in that market. It made her terrified since he'd taken them down in less than a minute or two.

The fact that he said his cousin was married to a human eased her fear slightly. He could be lying but he seemed sincere. Not that she was certain of that. She'd had zero personal interactions with aliens before being kidnapped. Pictures and vids didn't do them justice in real life. It had been her job to input data onto the computer archives of other races and thought she could identify most of them on sight.

None of the data she'd uploaded from the exploration teams had shown her someone like him. She'd been such a fool when she'd left Earth. It had sounded exciting to work on a research vessel and travel in space to learn about other worlds and cultures. She'd bought the bullshit propaganda about how advanced Earth weapons were compared to other alien races and how safe they'd be.

Those pirates had boarded *Bax* easily, which meant their space cannons hadn't destroyed the threat. The pirates had quickly overtaken their vessel and people had died. The aliens had ripped her away from everything she'd known in less than ten minutes from the time the first warning alarm had sounded until she'd found herself a caged prisoner.

27

"Please, Lilly." Raff's voice drew her from her thoughts. "Allow me to run the scan and give you medical treatment. Tell me how the Rexis got you. It will help distract you from your fear."

Her eyebrows shot up, almost offended at his suggestion. "Talking about the most traumatic experience in my life will lessen my fear? Do you really believe that?"

He scowled. "I'm not good with females. Or males for that matter. Talking isn't something I do often. I'm trying my best."

His last words resonated with her. She knew all about being in a situation well outside of her comfort zone. That had been her life after she'd left her family to go to school, later when she'd got a job in the city, and it had only gotten worse when she'd stepped foot on *Bax*. That was the vessel she'd spent six months and nine days on, before it had been attacked. Her co-workers had been vastly different from her and she'd felt like the odd man out. After the attack, she'd just known sheer terror.

"Please, Lilly."

He wanted to run a medical scan on her. Her face and lip hurt. So did her knee. She glanced back at the black mat thing. It was about two feet off the ground and reminded her of a rubber twin mattress. Only not since it appeared to be constructed out of charcoal. She hoped it was softer than it looked as she took a seat, pressing her thighs together and twisting a bit until she sat on the edge of it. Her behind sank into it and she was surprised that it felt cushioned. She couldn't help but tense as the Viking-cat like alien man slowly approached her. He really was scary and huge.

He crouched down with less than a foot of space between their bodies. The device in his hand wasn't something she'd ever seen before. Of course, not much alien technology was available on Earth and if it was, it sure wasn't in her price range to own. He gently used his free hand to take her wrist and pushed the cool metal against the inside of her arm just under her elbow.

"You'll feel a wet spray sensation but that will be all. Hold still. It won't hurt."

"What's it going to do?"

"Take a small sample of your blood to see what drug you were given."

She jerked a bit when the cold spray hit her skin but it was fast and painless. Her gaze locked with his golden eyes. His eyelashes were blond, matching his hair. They were thick and long. He really did remind her of a cat man though with the shape of them and the odd color they were. As strange as they looked, she really did find them mesmerizing. He was handsome for an alien. She tried to think of anything else besides his looks.

"Your cousin is really married to a human?"

"Yes. Cathian loves Nara. They are very happy together."

She let that sink in. Someone like him had married someone like her. She knew of at least two alien races that could breed with humans. The exploration teams had first found a human male married to a green alien female on the second planet they'd visited. Two children had resulted in their union. On the fourth planet, that team had met a human woman married to a big blue alien. They had a daughter.

It had been a hard thing to understand why a human would be attracted to an alien. Then again, she hadn't seen whatever Raff was before though. He was hot and kind of sexy, albeit a bit scary.

The device made a very low hum and he removed it from her arm, peering at it. Symbols flashed on a screen of the scanner but it wasn't a language she could read. Her gaze lifted to his face to watch his reaction. A low growl burst from him and he tapped the screen, scooting back a few feet.

"Am I contagious or something?" It was the first explanation that popped into her head with him inching away.

"No. They injected you with Narortion, probably to counteract the sleeping drug that is also in your system. Thankfully, it's only trace amounts or they could have killed you by overdose. I hate the Rexis." He sounded furious as he tapped the device with his finger, more like stabbing at it. He lifted it then, staring at her. "Hold still. I'm going to have it scan you for any wounds."

"It's just my lip, my face, and my knee."

"You could have internal injuries. Hold still."

She did but that didn't mean she couldn't ask questions. "What is Nortona or whatever you just said?"

A faint white light came out of the device. It had a wide beam. He pointed it just over her head. "Hold still. It's going to scan you."

She froze, not even daring to breathe, but she did close her eyes. A flash of white showed through her eyelids. The urge to peek became impossible to resist. He ran the light lower down her body, all the way to under her toes. He fell forward, going from a crouch to resting on his knees.

"What does it say?"

"It's processing the information. It will tell us in seconds."

"Was that light like an ultrasound?"

"I don't know that term. It will see your body on the outside and inside." The device made another hum and he lowered it, reading the display. That time he held still though, not retreating more. He finally looked up.

"Cuts and bruises but nothing serious." His golden eyes locked with hers. "You weren't sexually assaulted. I'm grateful for that. They didn't tag you with a tracker."

That first bit of information was something she already figured since she wasn't hurt to indicate someone had messed with her while she was drugged. The second part stunned her. "A tracker?"

"Yes. Some slavers install them to retrieve runaways." He rose to his feet, walked over to the med kit, and bent. He rummaged inside and held a small container when he straightened. "This will heal you. I can't do anything about the drugs in your system."

"You never told me what that drug is."

"I'm hoping the sedative, as little of it that remains in your bloodstream, will counteract the other."

He was avoiding her question and it pissed her off. "Look, Raif."

"Raff," he corrected, crouching in front of her.

"Raff. Sorry. My research vessel was attacked, I watched a few of my co-workers being murdered by aliens, and those bastards threw me into a cage. If that wasn't traumatic enough, they hit me with something that looked like a shock stick to knock me out every time I woke. I don't know where I am, what happened to the rest of the crew, or if I'm the only one who survived. I'm hoping that others were taken too and are still alive. I woke up to be told I'd been bought to work in a brothel and to take off my clothes because someone had paid to fuck me. I had to fight my way out of there and then, well, you know the rest. I just want you to tell me the truth. I deserve that. What was I given and am I going to die?"

Something close to sympathy softened his features. "You will not die. It's a drug given to stimulate activity in a person and make them feel good under bad situations."

She let that sink in. "Good? Can you be more specific?"

His gaze left hers. "Happy. Calmer. It dulls your fear in alarming situations."

She mentally reviewed what he said, trying to understand. "You're saying what they shot me with is like a happy pill? To change my mood?"

He nodded. "They must have given it to you in hopes of waking you more but they didn't want you to have negative moods when you became fully aware of your situation." He cocked his head. "You still fought them and escaped. I'm impressed."

"I'm not um, feeling happy. I'm just tired and feel a little drunk. It's probably from shock."

"Good." He held up the tiny bottle. "May I treat your injuries?"

She closed her eyes but nodded. It was all too much. Everything. The attack. Seeing her co-workers die when those aliens had shot them down in cold blood. One of the bastard aliens had grabbed her when she'd tried to run, tossed her over his shoulder, and taken her to a cage on another ship. The alarms on *Bax* had been blaring. She'd heard screams and people yelling. Her worst fear was that they'd murdered everyone but her. She wasn't sure how to live with that kind of guilt.

No, she told herself. *They stole me to sell to alien men. Those bastards had to have taken others too for that same purpose.* She wasn't important or special. Her job wasn't even vital. There had been four other data collectors on *Bax*. Even as far as being in shape and attractive, she was just average. Leslie, her team boss, would be the type of woman they'd want to sell. She was gorgeous, tall, and slender. Leslie had been on break when the attack happened. She had no idea what had happened to her. *Please don't let me be the only survivor. Please.*

A cool spray hit her lips and she startled.

"Easy. It will heal your injuries. Don't lick it. It won't harm you but it doesn't taste good."

She felt her skin tingle but it wasn't unpleasant. He sprayed some on her cheek next where she'd been hit. It was tough not to protest or jerk away when he moved her robe, exposing her knee. She opened her eyes to look down. Her skin there was scraped and bloody. He sprayed that too. It was amazing to watch as it began to heal in seconds.

"It works on humans."

"I see that." She forced her gaze up, staring into his golden eyes. "Thank you." He'd saved her. She understood that. "Once we're off this planet and your um, ship, comes, can you return me to Earth?"

He sighed, watching her, blinking. "No."

Panic hit. "Why not?"

"Earth is on a list of banned planets to visit."

"Why?"

"Most recently, they began to sell their females."

"That can't be true." She shook her head. "It's a lie."

"Talk to York's human female when we reach *The Vorge*. He's a crew member on my ship that is coming for us. Your Earth sold his Sara. She was taken from her work in one of your cities by your own kind and handed over to alien buyers."

The information stunned her. Was it possible the crew of *Bax* had been set up and sold their employees? It had been taken over quickly. She dismissed that suspicion though. The people she worked for had invested too much money into their research program. They wouldn't have done that. It wasn't cost effective. That's what it always came down to with big corporations.

"Try to relax. A shuttle will be here in the morning to pick us up, Lilly."

She wasn't certain if that should comfort her or not. At least she wasn't still in that brothel and Raff hadn't hurt her. He'd killed to protect her. The sight of all those hanging dead bodies in that marketplace area would give her nightmares. She'd almost ended up as one of them.

34

She touched her throat when it began to ache. Raff noticed, frowning.

Chapter Three

Raff made the female expose her neck to him. The material of her robe had hidden the red marks on it caused when Prix had grabbed her. Bruises would form soon if not treated. He sprayed her pale skin. Next, he studied her hands. They had a few tiny scrapes. They were so minor the handheld scanner had missed them. He took care of them as well.

"You're doing well, Lilly."

"It's hot in here."

His head snapped up to study her face. She looked a bit pinker than before in her cheeks and forehead. The cave was cool, not warm. Even with the bulky robe she wore, she shouldn't feel uncomfortable.

He had a bad feeling that the sedative might have just delayed the effects of the illegal stimulant that Lilly had been given to alter her mood. Some aliens died from it if they got overheated from their heart rate going too fast and their bodies overheated. He stood fast, worried. There were no drugs in the kit to help her and he was afraid to use another sedative to put her to sleep. Humans were frail creatures, probably easy to kill if given too many substances.

The pool caught his attention. "Bathe," he ordered.

Lilly stared up at him. "What?"

"You need to cool down. The water isn't cold enough to harm you but it should help. I have spare clothing inside my shuttle. My things will be large on you but I'm certain you might wish to get clean. Did the Rexis allow you to do that?"

"Rexis?"

"The aliens who were chasing you from the brothel and I'm certain they are also the ones who attacked your ship you spoke of. Were they the same?"

"Yes. Who are they?"

"Pirates. They have a habit of attacking all vessels." He didn't want to tell her that they tended to murder all the crew, normally focusing on the sale of the ships and merchandise they carried instead. That hadn't been the case with her but she was a human. He'd learned they sold for a good profit on the black market. It would have tempted the pirates to keep the females alive. "Were your crewmates all humans?"

"Yes." She stood and swayed on her feet.

Raff lunged forward to gently steady her. She didn't flinch away, allowing him to touch her arms.

"We were all from Earth. *Are*," she quickly amended. "Forty-eight onboard *Bax*, consisting of seven teams of five people each. Six exploration teams visited planets to collect data on the aliens who lived on them. My team recorded all the information. There *are* six bridge crew members and three security officers. All of them were also trained for maintenance and repairs. Two food workers. We also have a doctor and a nurse aboard."

It sounded as if her ship had been large to support that many humans. He led her toward the pool. It wasn't deep enough to be dangerous for her, even if she didn't know how to swim. "How many were females?"

"Does it matter?"

"Were you the only one?"

"No." She stopped at the edge of the pool, frowning at it. "It's moving."

"There's a slight current, yes. It's not strong." He pointed toward the left side of the pool. "Avoid that area. There's a waterfall that flows out of this cave. I doubt your body could accidently be swept down it since the opening is small but stay in this area. It's safe."

She shook her head. "What if there are alien fish? Do they eat people?"

Lilly amused him. "No fish or wildlife. At the top of the mountain is a lake formed by all the rain that is collected there. Water leaks down from it into this section through very tiny cracks. Nothing in there will harm you. The water is even drinkable."

She peered up at him. "What about you? Do you really expect me to strip off my clothes, few as I have, and trust you not to do something bad to me?"

It injured his pride that his word wasn't enough but he could understand her distrust. Lilly was smart and obviously a survivor. He respected that she'd fought her captors and even clawed at Prix with her tiny little finger claws. That took courage.

Eventually, she'd learn that he'd never do her harm and keep her safe at all costs. He found her very attractive but it wasn't the time to show his interest. She needed him to keep her safe until they reached *The Vorge*. Then he could pursue her in a sexual way.

He peered into her blue eyes, feeling a little guilt. Finding her had been lucky for him but the circumstances which brought her into his life had been the opposite for her. It wouldn't matter. He'd take care of her from that moment forward.

His male crewmates had each been fortunate to end up with human females. They made excellent companions. Cathian, York, and Dovis were content. Raff wanted the same thing. Lilly had literally fallen at his feet. The fact that she'd been shot by a stun blaster wasn't relevant. What was, he'd been there to save her. It had to be fate. She *would* become his.

"You can trust me, Lilly. Get clean. It will help with the drugs you've been given." He hoped. "I'll start a fire. You'll probably be cold when you get out. I'll get you clean clothing to wear. I would never force myself on you, Lilly. There's no honor in it. Your recent experiences have left you traumatized. In the words of some of the human females that live on my ship..." He paused, trying to remember exactly what Nara said often. "I look scary as fuck but I'm not a dick."

Her eyes widened.

"Was that correct? A person who treats others badly and isn't trustworthy?"

"Yes."

"I'm not one. I'm going to remove my shirt now. You'll need something to dry off with." He released her and backed off, pulling his shirt over his head, and tossing it at the edge of the pool.

She frowned, staring at his chest. "You wear shiny undershirts?"

He looked down. "It's armor that protects my vital organs."

"It doesn't look thick enough to do that." She reached out and her fingertips brushed against the fabric over his belly. "It feels like satin."

"I forget that Earth is so far behind with your technology. This will stop a blade or projectile from penetrating to my skin. It also will absorb one of those stun blasts you took to the back. One wouldn't have taken me down. Just irritated me."

She yanked her hand away. "That's amazing. We don't have that material back home. I mean, we have protective gear but it's bulky."

He silently promised to get her armor for under her clothing if she ever left *The Vorge*, once he got her there. He never wanted his future...he wasn't certain what to call her. His race life-locked to females. He couldn't form that kind of bond with one.

It didn't matter. He wanted Lilly and planned to keep her. Humans got married. He'd researched everything about Earth once Nara had come to Cathian.

Lilly felt sweat tickling down her back and between her breasts. Raff walked to the shuttle and climbed inside it. She turned away, debating the intelligence of trusting him. He had saved her life and if he'd wanted to rape her, he could have just done that. He looked strong enough to take what he wanted. Instead, he'd been a gentleman.

The idea of getting clean decided it for her. She began to strip off the rough textured, smelly robe. It had been horrifying to wake inside the cage after being taken from *Bax*, her uniform stripped from her body, only wearing her undergarments. At first she'd feared she'd been sexually assaulted but a quick examination of her body had assured her she hadn't been violated. It had been freezing cold in the cargo hold though and she'd huddled in her bra and panties, her teeth chattering. A guard had

40

come to check on her, perhaps she'd look pitiful enough to earn his sympathy, and he'd shoved the garment between the bars. She'd put it on and then he'd promptly knocked her out again with the shock stick weapon.

She went into the water in her undergarments. No way did she feel comfortable stripping bare. One glance toward the shuttle revealed Raff still inside. Maybe he was contacting that deep voiced Dovis again. The pool water was comfortable and only deep enough to rise to her ribcage. She sank down to her shoulders, using her hands to rub at her skin.

It helped cool her down. A slight noise drew her attention and she stared as Raff got out of the shuttle. He held folded clothing in one hand and some kind of small package his other. He avoided her gaze though, walked to the charcoal looking thing, and put the clothes down. He looked at her then, holding out the package.

"Soap and hair cleaner. May I approach?"

She nodded but backed away from the edge of the pool. He came closer, laid down what turned out to be a bag instead, and then straightened, giving her his back. She watched as he went to a large pile of wood and twigs in the far corner, got an armful, and dumped them into the firepit. He crouched in front of it and took something from his boot. Flames erupted seconds later and began to burn bright. He straightened again and returned to his shuttle, leaving her alone.

She opened the square bag and saw it contained what he said. At least she could identify the bar as soap. The other bottle contained green liquid. Maybe aliens didn't have shampoo *and* conditioner since there was only one. Raff remained with the shuttle, out of sight. She hesitated

41

before removing her undergarments. It was easy to use the soap to wash them. She rinsed the materials as best as she could, putting them on the pool ledge to dry. Then it was time for her to get clean.

Ten minutes later Raff exited the shuttle. He carried a large duffle bag with him. He dropped it near the fire, sat down on the charcoal seat, with his back to her.

"I have spare clothing for you next to me once you use my shirt to dry off, Lilly. I won't peek when you get out. There's also food if you're hungry. It's not much. Just emergency packets. I'd go hunting for fresh meat but the sun is going down. It's never a good idea to roam out there in the dark."

"Why?"

He hesitated. "This planet is called Gluttren Four, G4 for short. There are a lot of dangerous beasts that live here and it's too hot during the day for them to hunt for their food. They come out at night. We'd be considered a good meal to them."

That had her shuddering, imagining all kinds of dangerous creatures. "Can they attack us in here?"

"No. I told you about the imager shield."

She'd forgotten, glancing toward the entrance. The technology amazed her. They could see out but according to him, the opening would look and feel like solid rock to anyone on the other side.

She stared down at the water, suddenly no longer wanting to linger in it. He said the pool was fed by cracks in the mountain. What if an alien version of a snake or something similar slithered through? She moved fast to the edge, reached for the shirt he'd tossed there earlier, and grabbed it. Her gaze locked on his back as she climbed out.

"You won't peek?"

"You have my word."

She wasn't hot anymore. Shivers wracked her body as she tried to dry off. The material ended up very damp by the time she used it to wring out her wet hair. Raff didn't move, keeping his back to her. She quickly darted forward, grabbed the folded clothing he had next to him, and backed off.

She had to figure out what he'd given her. The short sleeve shirt was soft, huge, and tented her body. The pants reminded her of sweats, the way they had an elastic like waist, and the material thicker than the shirt. She had to bend, rolling the bottoms up to avoid walking on them. He had almost a foot of height on her and her legs were much shorter than his.

"I'm done." She rounded him and put her hands out toward the flames to get warm.

Raff scooted over. "We can share."

"I'm fine." She glanced at the rock floor but didn't want to sit there since she'd just gotten clean.

He sighed, his golden eyes narrowing. "I won't attack you, Lilly. Have a seat. Please. Are you hungry?"

She nodded. "Yes."

He bent forward, grabbed the larger bag, and opened it. He rummaged inside and came up with two packets. One looked like a kid's juice bag, only larger. The other reminded her of a sealed hot dog with its size and shape. He sat up straight and held them out to her.

What if he grabbed her? Her stomach rumbled with hunger. It had been at least a few days since she'd eaten. Maybe longer since she'd spent so much time unconscious. She again reminded herself that Raff appeared to be strong enough to do anything if he wanted to do her harm. That urged her to inch forward, sit on the farthest spot she could from him, and twist to take both packets.

"Thank you."

"This is vasia. It's a drink. Nutrients and water. It won't harm you. Cathian had all our emergency supplies replaced to be human digestion friendly."

She took the liquid packet.

"This is rishnia. It's close to a santwant."

She took it, frowning. She put the drink down, figured out how to unseal the wrapper on the food, and stared at it. "Sandwich. It looks kind of like one, if the bread were totally sealed closed. What's inside it?"

He shrugged. "Nara, my cousin's life-lock, said they aren't bad."

"It's not like I can be picky. I'm starving," she admitted, taking a bite.

The texture was similar to bread. Inside it had a paste filling that tasted like a meat mixture. Which ones, she couldn't determine. Maybe chicken and beef. She closed her eyes as she chewed and swallowed, grateful it was edible.

"Are you well?"

She took another bite, opened her eyes, and met his gaze. "I'm fine. This is good. Then again, I'd probably think cardboard was delicious after what I've been through."

"There are more rishnia packets if that doesn't fill you. All shuttles carry emergency supplies. *The Vorge* will reach us in about ten hours."

"What's your ship like?"

He hesitated. "*The Vorge* is a large vessel for an ambassador but we keep our crew number small."

She latched onto that. "Ambassador?"

"Cathian represents the Tryleskian people and their home world. We travel to different planets for goodwill, sometimes trade business agreements, and occasionally to prevent a war. It's why it's such a large vessel. It's not just a travel cruiser but battle ready in case we need to convince a potential enemy into rethinking that our race could be conquered or exterminated."

She ate, considering his words. It had been a huge honor to be hired onto *Bax*. Their mission had been to travel to discover new life and learn about alien cultures. The concept of going out there to meet aliens instead of waiting for whichever ones visited Earth had been huge news. According to Raff, it's what he did on his ship.

"How many planets have you been to?"

He shrugged. "Too many."

She was interested. "Like a few dozen?"

"Hundreds."

That blew her mind. "Wow. I had no idea there were that many. Aliens live on them? They all support life?"

"There are three habited planets in this solar system. Seven in the one I just came from. Four in the system before that. This surprises you?"

"Yes. We thought that maybe there might be a few dozen habitable planets in total. Only two alien races have visited Earth."

"Earth is in a remote system far from normal travel routes and the few scout reports that came in some years ago stated that you didn't have any technology that was trade worthy to make that trip. They also stated humans were quick to fear and attempted to murder off-worlders."

She let that sink in. "We're viewed as barbarians then?"

"Worse. It's one thing to attack someone who could be seen as an invader. Your people began to visit other planets. They haven't made good impressions with the ones they have."

"Why?"

He stared into the flames inside the fire pit. "The Yenisor incident comes to mind."

"What's that?"

He scowled, looking at her. "You don't know?"

She shook her head.

"Earth sent a ship there. It's one of the few habitable planets near yours. They are a peace-loving race. Non-aggressive. They are known for growing medical plants that cure many illnesses. Your people attacked them, bombed a few their settlements, and thousands died before help could reach them."

Horror filled Lilly and she found herself shaking her head. "No."

"Yes." Raff stared back at the flames. "The humans who went there demanded the Yenisors give them what they wanted or lives would be lost. When the Yenisors instead offered to trade with them for something of equal value, your people began to drop bombs, stating it would stop when they complied with their demands."

She felt sick. "What happened?"

"An allied race came to their defense. Some of the crops near those bombed settlements were destroyed. It effected the supply the Yenisors were able to send out to other planets in need of the lifesaving medicines created from those plants. More lives were lost. Everyone knows Earth was to blame. Now there is a battle ship stationed in orbit to protect their crops from humans returning."

"I didn't know. It was never on the news." She realized how stupid that sounded. "Of course, whoever was responsible would have covered that up. It wasn't like they would broadcast to everyone that they were being terrorists to aliens."

Raff nodded.

She wished the drink packet she had contained something stronger, like booze. Any time she heard really bad news, when shit hit the fan, that was her normal way to deal with it. A good stiff drink or four.

"That's another reason why I won't return you to Earth."

She yanked her head toward him, gaping.

"Your people will eventually piss someone off enough to cause a war or they might sell you to aliens. You're very attractive, Lilly. You could be bought by one of the races who would think of you as food or be forced to work in another brothel. I vow to keep you safe from this day forward. No one is ever going to hurt you again."

Lilly gaped at him but then closed her mouth. He sounded absolutely sincere. She wasn't sure if she should feel flattered or frightened.

"I need to um, my bladder." She peered at him.

He pointed. "Look behind the wood pile. There's a small cave in there with cracks in the floor."

She got up, worried. He suddenly removed a bracelet from his wrist, holding it out to her. She hesitated taking it. Raff touched it and a beam of light came out of it.

"Flashlight. Thank you."

He gave a nod.

She accepted it, making sure to avoid touching his fingers. The hole was there and it was a tiny cave she had to duck down to get inside. She understood what he meant when she saw the floor. Wide, foot long cracks splintered the uneven rock floor. She went closer to one, flashing the light into it. If it had a bottom, she couldn't see it.

She sighed loudly, put the oversized bracelet over her wrist, and glanced at the dark hole she'd entered through. Raff didn't follow her. She unfastened the pants and squatted.

"I wish caves came with toilets," she muttered.

It didn't take long and she returned, taking time to crouch near the water to do her best to wash her hands. The bracelet almost fell off. She returned it to Raff. He turned off the light and stood.

"We should get some sleep. I have an extra bed. You can take the mat where we sat. It will be more comfortable for you."

She watched him walk over to the shuttle and tried to relax. He was being good to her. *Things could be a lot worse. Like if I hadn't fought my way out of that brothel.* A shudder went down her spine.

Chapter Four

Raff jerked awake when his wrist alarm began to beep. He sat up on the inflatable bed he'd taken from the shuttle and quickly glanced at the camping mat Lilly slept on. He'd given her the blanket and another folded shirt to use for a pillow. The fire had almost died out but he could see her eyes were open, peering at him.

She sat up. "Is that your ship contacting you?"

He rose to his feet fast. "No. It's too soon. We've been sleeping less than an hour. Something else is out there. This is a proximity alert I set on the imager shield to warn me of any heat signatures." He made it to the cave entrance and snarled in fury. Four shuttles were out there, their search lights roaming the walls of the mountain above them.

Lilly gasped at his side. "Oh no."

One of the lights moved, hitting the barrier. He had to lift one hand to protect his eyes from being blinded by the strong beam. Lilly stumbled next to him. He moved on reflex, gripped her arm, and held her still.

"They can't see inside," he reminded her.

The light moved over and he lowered his hand. The four shuttles seemed to be searching every inch of the mountain. His mind worked fast and he snarled again. He'd checked Lilly for a tracker. He sure as hell hadn't been tagged. The force field on his shuttle would have prevented anyone from attaching one to the hull when it had been parked.

How did they seem to know where they were? It was obvious they were searching for a cave entrance. They'd have been found if it wasn't for the imager device. It not only provided cover to hide them but emanated a signal to confuse life sign readings. Their pursers shouldn't have known where they were unless...

"Fuck." He released her and rushed to his shuttle, turning on the interior lights. It took time to locate what had penetrated his hull. He glared at the hard-shelled capsule.

"What is it?" Lilly had followed him.

He turned and showed her. "Tracker." It infuriated him. Someone had encased the device to breach the hull of his shuttle. It would be tough to destroy but he needed to cut the signal. He bent, pulling one of his guns from his boots, and set the tracker down on a rock to fire at it.

"Wait!" Lilly grabbed at his arm.

"They could start bombing the mountain to bring it down around us when they can't find a way to reach us. The tracker tells them we're somewhere here." His gaze went to the cave entrance. They could try to flee but the other shuttles were almost on top of them. They'd be shot down within seconds.

Lilly released him, bent, and snatched up the tracker. She ran away from him. He spun, confused. "What are you doing?"

She grabbed a bunch of thin sticks and rushed toward the pool. "You said there's a current and the water inside here goes down a waterfall, right? Takes the water away from the cave?"

He followed her as she dropped to her knees. "Yes."

"What's the size of the waterfall opening?"

51

She grabbed one of her small white pieces of clothing she'd left on the edge of the pool, wrapping it around the tracker. Then she bundled the sticks to surround it.

He crouched down, watching her with a scowl. "What are you doing?"

"Answer me!" She reached up, grabbing the second piece of small clothing she'd left there. She wound it around the bundle, tying the ends of it together. "Is it too small for this raft to float through?"

Her plan became clear. "That's brilliant. It will fit. You've made a raft of sorts for the tracker. Why the clothing?"

"The tracker is bullet sized. I didn't want it to slip through the sticks. I wrapped it in my underwear in the center."

"How did you think to do this?"

"Easy. I hated going fishing when I was a kid. I used to float worms away in the river on little twig and plant vines rafts I built when my dad made me go with him. Those were what he used for bait. I also figured I might be saving their lives, which was a bonus. The fewer the worms left in the bucket, the faster I got to go home." She paused. "My bra should hold all the sticks together so it doesn't fall apart and drop the tracker. We don't want it to sink." She picked up the bundled sticks, handing it to him. "Will this make it through the waterfall hole?"

He took it, studying what she'd done. "Yes." He rushed to the far side of the pool and leaned over the water, dropping it. It landed, went under, but then floated to the top. The slight current was stronger near the drop and it began to flow that way. He turned on his wrist light, aiming it for the bundle. He watched it go over and fall out of sight.

The waterfall would flow to the canyon floor and then into the ground cracks there that fed into an underground river. He spun, rushed past Lilly, and back to the opening of the cave. The four shuttles were still hovering just outside, their search lights in motion. Lilly came up to his side. He turned off his wrist light. The longest minutes of his life passed but then the shuttles began to move away toward the other side of the mountain.

"It's working, isn't it?"

He turned and smiled Lilly. "Yes." He felt proud of her quick thinking. It made him want her more. He acted without giving it thought by reaching for her. Her black hair was softer than it appeared when he gently cupped her face and head, leaned down, and planted a kiss on her lips. She had soft, pliable ones.

Her mouth parted slightly when she gasped. He liked it when her hands flattened on his shirt but she didn't push him away. Instead she seemed to just want to feel him. He ran the tip of his tongue along the seam of her lower lip and deepened the kiss. Her hands fisted in his shirt.

He would stop if she tried to twist her face to the side or push him away but she didn't. It encouraged him to swipe his tongue with hers She leaned into him, kissing him back. Little moans came from her. Desire shot through his body lightning fast, straight to his shaft. She tasted sweet, probably from her meal, but he liked it.

He released the side of her head, sliding his fingers of that hand out of her hair and reached down, getting a good hold on one side of her ass. It felt soft and nice to squeeze. He pulled her short body even closer to his, released her ass, and wrapped his arm around her waist. Humans were fragile. He needed to remember that as he lifted her higher up his body.

She twisted her head, breaking the kiss, and he froze. Her eyes opened and he stared deeply into them. They were foreign but beautiful. That light shade of blue was quickly becoming his favorite.

"Shit."

Her whispered word had him wondering if she was about to begin fighting and demand he put her down. She surprised him instead by releasing her tight grip on his shirt and sliding them up to his shoulders.

"What are we doing?" She glanced at his lips, before gazing back into his eyes.

"Celebrating your intelligence." He smiled. "That was my first kiss. How was it?"

Her eyes grew bigger and her lips parted. He went for her mouth again. It seemed like an invitation to him. She closed her eyes and didn't flinch away.

He kissed her again, deeply. He remembered what Cathian had told him about how he'd accidently cut Nara a few times with his fangs, being careful to not apply any pressure with them when her tongue touched the pointed tips.

The ground under his feet suddenly thumped and a split second later, a distant blast reached his ears. He was the one to end the kiss that time, staring around the cave. Small bits of dust fell from a few of the cracks above them where the smoke from the fire usually drifted up through the mountain to keep it from filling the enclosed area.

He reacted fast, jerking Lilly higher up his body. They needed to leave. He spun, running toward the shuttle. At the open door, he gently dumped her inside.

"Stay put. They are bombing!"

He ran to where he'd put his bag, leaving the other things where they were, and rushed back to the shuttle. He threw the bag into the storage area, reached for a stunned Lilly still sitting where he'd put her, and lifted her. His ass hit the seat and he dropped her onto his lap. He sealed the door, flipping on the engines.

"What's going on?" She sounded panicked.

"The tracker must have gotten caught up somewhere or they realized it is in the water." To verify his guess, another bomb hit the mountain. More debris and a few small chunks of rock rained down outside the shuttle. One piece struck it. The sound of the blast was too muted to hear inside.

He pushed her forward and put on his belts. Then he pulled her back against his chest. "They are too close and might be able to shoot us down. We're going to have to fly out of here fast." He didn't want to frighten her but he needed her cooperation. "Reach down and hold on tight to the sides of the seat. If we're hit and need to eject, I'll grab hold of you. I won't let go."

"Eject?" Her voice rose to a high pitch that made him wince.

He flipped on the night vision screen since he didn't want any exterior lights to broadcast their location and stared straight ahead, gripping the thrusters with one hand, the steering control with the other.

"Hold on," he rasped. "Trust me."

He gently lifted them off the cave floor and eased forward.

"We're going to hit the shield thing! Can't we just stay here?"

He didn't want to state to her that the bombs would collapse the cave and crush them, even inside the shuttle. "We can fly through the imager shield. It's only solid from the outside. It means I can't reverse us back in once we're out." He meant that as a joke but she didn't laugh. His crewmates were probably right. He didn't have a sense of humor.

He flew them out of the cave and down, going slow to avoid slamming into the rock overhang. Once they neared the canyon floor, he spotted at least two shuttles hovering higher to his far left. He turned his shuttle to the right and hit the thrusters hard. It shoved Lilly's small body against his. All his attention went to avoiding slamming them into the canyon walls and the floor as he picked up speed.

"Hold on," he repeated. He couldn't make a mistake. The small female sitting on his lap would die if he crashed. Either from the impact or by the ones in the other shuttles seeking them to return her to Prix.

Solid rock, trees, and ground flew past them far too close. Lilly kept her eyes tightly closed to avoid watching as the crazy hot kisser alien drove his shuttle at super speed through the canyon. The feeling of motion was making her nauseous as he dodged and weaved.

Not a time to puke, she kept repeating in her head.

Her fingers hurt from where they gripped the sides of the seat. Raff had told her to hang on and she was. For dear life. It got worse when the shuttle suddenly went vertical, then shooting straight upward. She opened her eyes, instantly regretting it. All she could see was blackness through the glass front of the shuttle.

An alarm began to blare. She closed her eyes again, released the seat, and dug her hands under Raff's thighs instead. He adjusted his body a little to help her wedge more of her fingers between the underside of his legs and the seat.

"Is that an engine stall warning?" She'd always hated to fly and feared something like that happening on Earth.

"No. They have targeted weapons at us."

Why did I ask? Why? She whimpered, expecting to be blown up at any second.

The shuttle began to level off, before it veered severely to the right. The speed alone they were flying at kept her pressed against Raff but she could tell they were almost completely sideways. Didn't he have gravity stabilizers? *Bax* had them. Then again, it had been a huge vessel and never adjusted course as fast as Raff did. They veered left next. The alarms went silent.

She opened her eyes. It was still dark out there. She glanced up and saw another screen practically on the roof of the shuttle. It looked more like a computer game with digital cartoon imaging but she got the gist. It was telling them where the ground was, which looked far away, and showed some upcoming mountains. They looked massively tall. Raff flew straight toward them.

He reached up, touching the area next to that screen, and another one lit up. Four dots showed.

"What are those?"

"Our pursuers."

"We didn't lose them?"

"No. We're faster than they are though."

"We're going to be okay then?"

He dove them toward the ground. "Yes. I won't let anything happen to you, Lilly."

She desperately wanted to believe him. They almost hit the ground, flying super low, but he dodged large rocks and trees. Maybe he was doing it to avoid the other shuttles' radar. He flew them into another canyon between the mountains and they veered left. She watched, realizing he was rounding the mountain.

"Why are you going back the way we came?"

"Losing them and returning close to where the cave is. It's the last place they'll look."

She hoped that was true. Her gaze drifted up. There were no more dots on the second screen. Raff flew low, close to the ground. Another mountain range came into view, this one much smaller than the last. That had to be where their cave had been. He slowed the shuttle when they got closer and lowered it to the ground between two large rocks.

"What are we doing?"

He shut down the engines, reached up, and his fingers flew over a control pad to the right. "Becoming one with the rock next to us." He dropped his hand to the console to his right, tapping in more commands. He finally sighed and his tense body relaxed.

She turned her head, peering up at him in the dim interior lighting. His golden gaze met hers. A small smile teased his lips.

"We're safe. The protective shield is up. We'll read on their sensors as part of these two boulders and we'll visually look like an extension between them if they run search lights over the area."

She let that sink in. "What now?"

"We wait until *The Vorge* sends a shuttle for us in the morning."

Chapter Five

Lilly shifted her behind on Raff's lap. Something dug into part of her butt. She hadn't noticed before since she'd been too afraid they'd crash or be shot from the sky. It didn't help much since now something dug into the edge of her thigh. He was a big guy but it made for cramped sitting options with only one seat to share.

"What's wrong?"

She sat up and reached down, feeling his pants where her ass had been, and feeling something hard. "What's in your pants?" She made the mistake of glancing over her shoulder at him and found him giving her a look she could identify. Amusement. "I guess men are the same regardless of what planet they are born on. I'm talking about this." She gave it a tug.

"One of my blades. There are bunch of them strapped to me and I have a few hidden pockets."

"What about this?" She reached for what had been irritating her leg, found another hard source under the material.

"Dagger."

She remembered when he'd saved her. "How many weapons do you keep in your pants?"

He chuckled.

"Stop twisting my words into something dirty. I'm not talking about your dick. You're lumpy to sit on. I didn't notice before when I've ended up on your lap because we've been running for our lives both times."

"Many."

"Can you remove them?" She leaned to the side a little, staring at the area behind his seat. "Maybe I can sit back there."

"No. I'm going to convert the seat. I can't do that if you're in the storage area."

"Convert?"

"This is a single flyer space shuttle. Pilots need sleep eventually. No one can stay up for an eight-day flight, which is the max capability of this model. The seat straightens into a bed."

She frowned, thinking about that. "What do you do if you need to pee?"

He pointed toward a side panel in the back. "Hand held device that suctions waste away."

Her mouth fell open but she closed it fast.

"Do you need to use it? We can't leave the shuttle or open the door. It's simple. You just press the cupped area between your legs, go, and then press a button. It will wash and dry you."

"I'm good."

She shifted on his lap again. Something dug into her. She ran her hands down the side of his leg, feeling the weapons. They seemed to be hidden in his pants all down his thighs to his knees, where she stopped feeling.

Raff arched a single eyebrow at her exploring him. She stopped.

"Sorry. You're lumpy to sit on, as I said."

"Stand up."

There was a tiny space between the seat and the door. She scooted off his lap and had to keep bent somewhat to avoid hitting the roof with her head. Once she was off his lap, he bent forward, removing his boots. He set them against the wall. Then he leaned back, his hands going for the front of his pants.

"What are you doing?"

"Removing them."

Her mouth hung open again as he unfastened his pants, lifted his hips, and shoved them down. She saw a flash of skin before she closed her eyes, turning her head. "You're not wearing underwear!"

"I never do."

"You can't expect me to sit on your naked lap."

He chuckled. She listened to clothing rustling and then he gripped her hips with both hands, twisted her, and she landed on his lap again. This time sideways. Her arm hit his bare chest and her eyes flew open. He'd not only removed his pants but his shirt too. She gaped at his muscular chest and all that tan skin revealed. He had nipples, like a human guy did, but no chest hair.

"Look down."

She couldn't refuse, curious, and realized he'd used his shirt to cover his lap. It effectively put a barrier between them. Lilly swallowed hard. She was still shocked that he had stripped everything off.

"Better?"

She peered into his eyes. "You're naked."

"Yes. Ready to get some sleep?" He reached to the side, tapping in a command.

"You want to sleep? After what just happened?"

"Do you want to kiss me again?" He grinned. "We could do that."

She swallowed hard. Him kissing her had been surprsing but it had been pretty amazing at the same time. Probably the best kissing she'd ever experienced. If those bombs hadn't begun to drop, there was no telling what would have happened between the two of them. She might not have wanted him to stop.

"Sleeping is good," she finally said, deciding it was a safer alternative than making out with a hot alien.

"That's what I thought. We need some rest."

She gasped as the seat lifted them both into part of the storage compartment. The back of the seat flattened and a section rose where his legs were to support them. The chair did turn into a bed. She would have slid off him to hit the wall but supports rose on each side, creating a kind of barrier. She ended up laying sideways against him.

"Get comfortable." He adjusted his body under hers. "You might want to face me more. I'm your bed." He released her with one arm and touched something to the side. The lights lowered until she could barely see him.

Her cheek was pressed against his hot, firm skin. She could hear the steady drum of his heartbeat. The guy had a million muscles too. She felt them when he'd shifted his position under her a little.

"You really expect us to sleep like this?"

"It's going to be at least five hours before the sun rises. Then a few more before *The Vorge* reaches orbit and sends down a shuttle. We could get to know each other better."

She was pretty sure that was a sexual innuendo if she ever heard one. It was the way his voice turned huskier than normal. She flattened her hand on his chest near her face to brace against and lifted a bit, staring at him.

Those golden eyes were watching her, a predatory look in them. Her gaze went to his mouth, remembering how he'd kissed her. Twice. She also had time to ask the question she'd wanted to before everything had turned crazy and they were rushing toward the shuttle to leave the cave.

"You never kissed anyone before?"

"Never."

Her gaze traveled down to his chest and his broad shoulders, thickly muscled arms, before studying his handsome face. He was really good looking for a Viking/lion man. "Have you ever had sex?"

"Many times."

She was confused.

"Kissing is intimate."

Lilly frowned. "And sex isn't?"

He held her gaze. "I've only fucked brothel workers and used protection to prevent them from giving me diseases. I never allowed them to touch me or took off my clothing to go skin to skin with them." He paused. "I bent them over in front of me, unzipped, and covered my shaft with a protection barrier."

He was clear about details at least. "Never anything else?"

He hesitated. "I tried feeding from a few females when I was younger. They weren't brothel workers though. My mother warned me I'd need their hormones. It didn't work and it turned out I wasn't as Tryleskian as we feared."

"I don't understand."

He took a deep breath and blew it out. "My father is Tryleskian and I physically took after him. My mother was Pina, Rornior, Scatia, and Minleor."

She frowned, confused. "I've near heard of those alien races."

"They came from a solar system of a dying sun. They fled when their planets were becoming unstable, pooling their resources to save as many lives as possible. It meant they bred together on shared ships and finally ended up here. No civilized planet wanted to take them in a hundred and forty years ago. That's when they settled here. Only a few thousand in all made it this far. Not all the ships survived the journey."

"That's so sad. Why wouldn't anyone take them in?"

"They spent five generations on those ships traveling from their solar system to find a home here. The first generation had a hard time mingling and getting along with other races they shared ships with. Their leaders agreed to make it law to mate with someone of another race to create harmony and peace. There was no need to fight if they merged their DNA. By the fifth generation, they had succeeded. There were no full blooded Pina, Rornior, Scatia, or Minleor left. A lot of planets believe it's a crime to purposely do something like that. You've been in the city and seen a lot of their descendants. They don't look similar, taking traits from those four

65

races and others that have settled here. A lot of cultures aren't into mixing races. They are viewed as atrocities when their bloodlines are that mixed."

"That's so wrong."

"It is. That's why my father refused to claim my mother. He probably feared she'd never be accepted on his planet and I know he was embarrassed that I resulted in their union."

She frowned, confused.

"He crashed on G4 and was stuck here for months. Tryleskian males need to feed off female hormones when their heat hits every three years. He was on his way home knowing his heat was coming to reach females of his own race. He fed from my mother instead and when his brother sent a rescue ship, my father abandoned my pregnant mother. She raised me on her own. We believed I completely took after my father and that I'd go into heat when I hit adulthood. My mother instructed me to feed from females, hoping it would start my heat cycle. It failed."

Her attention focused on his mouth. His fangs reminded her of a Vampire. "You tried to drink their blood?"

"No." He snorted. "To feed off a female is intimate." He licked his lips. "It is to use my lips and tongue to greatly arouse and make them feel immense pleasure. That's how I feed. I need the hormones they produce."

Her mouth parted as she figured out what he was saying. "Oh." He went down on women. She felt her body respond and it slightly embarrassed her but Raff was a super sexy alien. He was also naked, she was laying on him, and touching his warm, bared chest. Her mind totally went there imagining what it would be like if he wanted to feed off her.

66

His nostrils flared and a low growl came from him. It made his chest vibrate under her. "Humans are compatible with Tryleskiars." His golden eyes slightly narrowed and his voice lowered. "Let me feed from you."

Her cheeks heated, she figured she was blushing badly, and her heart pounded.

"You'd enjoy it," he huskily whispered.

She had human men hit on her often. To get women into bed seemed a normal pastime for all men. Anyone with breasts became a target on Earth. She'd even had that happen on *Bax*. Raff wasn't just some guy though. Not even close. She felt flustered, uncertain how to react to his blatant request, and tongue tied.

He suddenly wrapped an arm around her waist and lifted his body up, turning them both in the small space. She gasped and grabbed hold of his shoulders when he did. She ended up under him and with him on top of her.

"Raff!"

He slid his arm out from under her, reached over to touch something on the wall, and the sides of the bed lowered. He moved down, straddled it, and gripped her legs. He was strong as he bent them upward, putting her feet on his warm chest. He held her gaze as he reached for the waist of her pants, unfastening them.

"We have hours to wait. I'll stop if you don't enjoy it."

She should have fought, twisted away, but she couldn't look away from his intense golden stare. She was curious and more than a little turned on. This...alien...had saved her life. She trusted him. Raff could have hurt her a dozen times or more but hadn't.

He opened the pants she wore and began to pull them down her hips. With her legs bent, he worked them down her legs to her ankles. She hesitated when he stopped and then lifted her feet off his chest. He tore the pants off completely, tossing them to the side.

His gaze left hers and he gripped her thighs with his big, warm hands, and pushed them apart. She didn't protest. He didn't hesitate to lower his head as his hands slid upward until he held her inner thighs, pinning her down. She did close her eyes though, not willing to watch him. She'd only had a guy go down on her once. It had been awkward and she hadn't enjoyed it. Her second boyfriend liked to lick everywhere except her clit. She wondered if Raff would be the same.

His hot breath fanned her pussy and then she jolted when his thick, wet tongue slid along her clit. She sucked in a sharp breath and her eyes opened, staring at the ceiling of the shuttle. He did it again and again. She bit her lip, biting back a moan. He knew where her clit was, focused on it, and it felt really good.

She grabbed at the side of the chair/bed and dug her nails into the material. Raff began to growl and lick at her faster, adding vibrations into the mix. She couldn't hold back anymore, small moans coming from her. He was amazing at...feeding. He was going at her like a starved person too.

The pleasure became intense and she couldn't take it, trying to squeeze her legs closed. Raff's hands gripped her inner thighs tighter, holding her open. She bucked her hips but he pinned her down. His growling increased. It probably would have scared her, it was a terrifying sound, but those vibrations ended up sending her over the edge.

"Raff!" She yelled his name as she came hard, her mind feeling as if it were going to explode from the intense climax.

He stopped licking her clit and lowered his mouth. She almost whimpered when his tongue traced her slit and then he pushed it inside her pussy. She clawed at the material and panted. He had a thick tongue that worked its way inside her a few inches and then he withdrew it. Her body went limp until he did it again, slowly fucking her that way.

"Oh god." She threw her head back.

He withdrew his tongue. "So good, Lilly."

His voice was deeper than she'd ever heard it, huskier. She relaxed, still breathing hard. She lifted her head, staring down at him. He'd raised his head too, peering at her from between her legs. His eyes were incredibly sexy. He broke their gazes and resumed licking at her clit. She tried to buck away, feeling oversensitive, but he pinned her down.

"Too soon," she cried out.

He didn't stop licking her, making her take the almost pained pleasure. He had no mercy. She released the sides of the chair and slid her fingers into his thick hair, lightly raking her fingernails on his scalp. The texture of his hair was nice but different from anything she'd ever felt. Thicker but soft. He began to almost snarl, causing a different kind of vibration coming off his tongue. Lilly moaned loudly, unable to hold back, and panted. The second time he made her come had her screaming his name again.

He ran his tongue down her slit but then lifted up, releasing her thighs. She stared down at him. His expression appeared harsh, almost as if he were enraged.

69

"What's wrong?"

"Nothing. Everything is right." He grabbed at his waist, threw the shirt he'd kept over his lap to the side, and suddenly gripped her hips. He jerked her down the flat surface closer to him. "You belong with me, Lilly. Now and forever."

Her mind felt a little slow, probably from having her brain fried twice by his tongue, but she tried to make sense of what he was saying. He slid his hands under her knees, lifted her legs up, and then yanked her closer. Something hard and thick pressed against her pussy and she realized it was his cock.

He leaned forward, coming down on her, and released her legs. "Wrap around me. Now."

She hesitated.

His mouth went for hers. She closed her eyes and opened up to him. She could taste herself on his tongue when it delved into her mouth. Raff could kiss. He reached between the small space between their chests and tore at the borrowed shirt she wore. Material ripped and she realized she was a little sweaty when air hit her now exposed skin. He cupped one of her breasts, giving it a squeeze.

She wound her arms around his neck. He let go of her breast and came down on top of her until his upper body pinned hers. He reached down, hooked one of her legs, and pulled it up to the side of his hip. She understood and wrapped her legs around him.

He lifted a little, adjusted his hips, and then she felt his cock nudge her pussy. He felt really thick and it scared her. He was going to fuck her. She broke the kiss, twisting her head a little, and opened her eyes.

He peered into hers from inches away, the golden of them so close she could take in every detail. His pupils were slightly slanted instead of round. There were streaks of lighter gold in the irises. Raff had beautiful eyes.

"Accept me," he rasped.

"Raff, I…"

"You're mine, Lilly. I'm yours. Don't deny us both."

She wanted him. "Gentle. You feel huge."

His lips slightly curved in a smile. "Gentle," he agreed.

She relaxed, letting her hands touch his back where they were wound around his neck. His skin was firm and hot. She loved the feel of it under her fingertips and palm. He nudged her pussy with his cock and slowly pushed forward.

She stared into his eyes, knowing hers widened at the feel of her body resisting taking something that thick. She was wet though, had come twice, and he pressed against her more.

Her body gave and the broad tip of his cock began to enter her. A low rumble of a growl came from Raff, his chest vibrating against her breasts that were smashed between them. He pushed in more.

Lilly dug her nails into his back, adjusting her legs a little higher around his waist. He was big. She could feel herself stretching tight around the girth of his cock. She hadn't even seen what he looked like down there before having sex with him.

Probably for the best or I'd be afraid right now, she silently admitted.

He was rock hard as he pushed into her deeper. He froze there, withdrew a little, and pushed back in. A moan broke from her at the sensation. He felt huge but really good. There was no pain.

Raff worked his way inside Lilly's tight, wet pussy with small, gentle strokes. She took him a little at a time. He had to use every bit of control he had. She felt amazing. There was no protection barrier over his shaft. It was just her and him. The ecstasy she gave him was enough to make him want to shoot his seed inside her deep. He held off though, wanting it to be good for her first.

He couldn't get over how tight she was around his shaft. Human males must be small or perhaps Lilly hadn't ever been with a male. She was too beautiful though for him to believe he'd be her first. Many males must have pursued her.

He loved the little moans she made, the way her dull finger claws raked across his back, kneading into his skin. She tightened her grip around his hips as he lifted his legs onto the bed to get better traction to rock his hips into the cradle of her thighs.

He felt relief when he fully buried his shaft into the tight confines of her pussy. She could take all of him. He understood now why his crewmates and cousin had bonded to humans. Lilly was his. It wasn't just how much pleasure she gave him. He'd felt protective of her since the moment he'd seen her and those feelings had deepened. The way her body responded to his, her taste when aroused, and even the sounds she made just cemented the need to keep her forever.

He let go of some of his control and allowed his Rornior trait to come forward. He'd learned about it the first few times he'd gone to brothels. As much as he'd taken after Tryleskians, he had realized soon enough he had parts of his mother's bloodlines too.

He felt pressure in his groin, releasing holding it back, and Lilly gasped. Her dull finger claws dug deeper into his skin. She might even make him bleed. He didn't care if she did. It was a good kind of pain. The vibrations that started at the top of his shaft turned him on more. Lilly jolted under him and her legs squeezed him.

"What..."

He took her mouth, kissing her, to silence her questions as he began to slowly fuck her in deep, long strokes. She moaned against his tongue, almost screaming as he picked up the pace. He ground the top of his cock against her clit with each thrust of his hips.

Lilly tore her mouth from his, screaming. Her pussy clamped tight around his shaft. He had to fight to keep moving as he felt her inner muscles fluttering, milking him. She thrashed under him and he gave into his body's demands. A roar tore from him as his seed shot through his shaft and deep inside her pussy. He lost the ability to think, only feeling every drop of it surging forward and causing him to experience the most intense euphoria of his life.

He realized his body had gone lax and he braced his arms, making certain to not crush Lilly under him. They were both breathing hard. He smiled, studying her face. She had her eyes closed, her lips parted, and her skin a light pink shade. She seemed to notice his attention and opened her eyes, meeting his. He grinned.

She surprised him when she pulled her hands off his back and cupped his face. "Wow."

He liked the way she stroked him. One of her thumbs lightly traced his lower lip. "We're perfect together, Lilly."

"What was that?"

"Sex between us."

She appeared flustered, her cheeks pinkened more, and she released his face to settle her hands on his chest. He knew what she wanted to know. All the brothel workers had asked the same question on other worlds. Just not G4 since other males with Rornior traits had the same sexual ability.

"Never mind." She glanced away from him.

"I like to tease you, Lilly." He used his finger to stroke her cheek, adjusting his weight over her.

She met his gaze again, holding it.

He refused to pull his shaft out of her body. He liked being inside her, a part of her, with them intimately joined. "When I'm highly turned on and close to losing my seed, a swelling happens at the top of my shaft near the base. It only comes out then and it caused the pulsation you felt."

Her eyes widened. "You turn into a vibrator there. It was like…"

"Yes."

"Wow." She licked her lips. "That's really amazing. We have sex toys on Earth." Her cheeks turned a little pinker. "Shit. Not that you're a sex toy but that felt amazing."

"Sex between us will always be good and we'll both enjoy it immensely."

She seemed to search his eyes with hers.

"What is it, Lilly? You may ask me anything. We're joined forever."

She looked surprised. "Forever?"

"I didn't use a barrier on my shaft. Forever."

Her hands splayed on his chest and her breathing increased. He was pretty sure that was panic he saw flash across her features. He smiled. She was human and didn't know much about other races. It wasn't true but he wasn't about to ever tell her that. She was his. He was keeping her.

"We're bonded. You're mine. I'm yours. Forever."

"That can't be. You mean like...married?"

Panic sounded in her voice. He smiled wider. "Yes."

She pushed on his chest. Not that she was strong enough to move him. She wasn't. "That can't be."

"It is. I asked if you accepted me. You did."

"I didn't know!"

He leaned in and kissed her. She only resisted for a split second before accepting his kiss and returning it. He loved her mouth and her pink little tongue. It was soft and sweet. He pulled back, gazing into her eyes.

"I'll be good to you, Lilly. Your happiness is a priority. So is your pleasure." He slowly began to move inside her, his shaft hardening again.

She clutched at him, a soft moan coming from her parted lips. Her legs tightened around his hips. He arched his back a little to reach her throat when she threw her head back, tasting her skin there and giving open mouthed kisses. He lightly nipped her with his fangs and a louder moan came from her.

"Your pleasure is my pleasure, Lilly."

"Oh god. You're going to kill me, Raff."

He chuckled as she began to buck her hips in tune with his, urging him to fuck her a little faster. "No, my little human. Never that but I do plan to make you come again and again."

Chapter Six

Lilly woke, sprawled naked on top of Raff. He'd put the sides of the bed up after he'd nearly fucked her into oblivion and settled them for the night to get some sleep before morning.

Every detail returned to her memory. She'd had sex with the big predatory Viking lion man at least four times, plus the two times he'd gotten her off with his mouth. And they had been the best orgasms she'd ever experienced in her entire life. Above and beyond anything she could have ever imagined or hoped for. His soft snores had woken her.

She opened her eyes. The interior of the shuttle was still dark but faint light showed from the front, enough for her to make out the chest under her cheek. Raff's arms were wrapped around her. One of his hands rested on her ass, the other at the small of her back. She was straddling his waist, her legs resting against the outside of his.

She lifted her head, peering at Raff. His eyes were closed. He didn't look near as dangerous when he slept, his features lax. He was handsome. There was no denying that she was attracted to him like she'd never been before to any man she'd ever met. It didn't seem to matter that he was an alien. She wasn't sure if that should worry her or not.

They were married, basically. At least that's what he'd implied. They hadn't really talked about it since he'd cut their discussion off by fucking her. It was probably for the best since she'd certainly started to freak out.

The Enderlings, a race the research team had come into contact with on one of the planets, mated for life with their first sexual partner. She'd thought that romantic when she'd read over their reports and entered the data. They didn't cheat as a race, committing to each other until death. As it had been explained, the male's sperm acted almost like a DNA sequencer on the female, physically making her only receptive to him. And vise versa. They could only have children together. Her body would reject sperm from another male. They could only feel arousal toward each other too.

Was Raff like that? Had his sperm changed her on a physical level? She didn't feel any different. Just slightly sore between her legs and tired. Both of those things made sense though since he was a big guy and she figured she hadn't slept long.

A soft growl startled her and she turned her head. There was something outside of the shuttle window in the front. Something big. It moved closer. It was too dark to make out the details but whatever it was, it wasn't her imagination. The shadow moved again.

"Raff," she whispered.

He kept sleeping. She gripped his shoulder, giving it a shake. His snoring stopped and his body tensed under hers. She looked at him and found his eyes open now as he gazed at her.

"There's something outside." She kept her voice low.

He moved his hands. One arm locked around her waist, the other reaching for the side of the shuttle. The bed began to move. She clutched at him. The back of it rose up and they shifted toward the front. He was transforming it back into a seat. She watched his face since she'd already established she couldn't make out what was outside the shuttle. His expression hardened as he stared forward.

"Damn. A fasis. Be quiet," he breathed softly. "They have excellent hearing."

She twisted her head when the bed became a seat. It had left her straddling his lap, sitting on top of him. The big shape was easier to see that close to the front window of the shuttle and she reached up, pressing her hand over her mouth to smother a gasp.

The beasty animal was the size of transport bus on Earth. Maybe fifteen feet high and thirty feet long. She squinted, trying to make out more details. It looked like something between a huge turtle and an elephant. The head of it turned and she saw a series of long tusks, maybe ten or so. They stuck out like deadly spikes by a good six feet in length.

"Shush," Raff wrapped his arms around her waist, pulling her tighter against his chest. "It can't see us. The shuttle looks like the rock."

She remembered that. She swallowed hard and lowered her hand. "Is it deadly?"

"Very. Most beasts on G4 are. They can move fast, stab their prey with their spikes, and then feed while it's trapped there."

"It can't pierce the shuttle though, right?"

Raff said nothing, his focus on the front window.

Her heart sank, figuring that answered her question. It could. Raff released her and reached up, tapping something. The window changed slightly, some kind of filter coming on, showing her the terrifying beast in vivid detail.

It didn't so much resemble a turtle but maybe an armadillo and an elephant combined. It had shell platting over its large body, a small tail, and those spikes looked sharp at the tips, a few inches thick. It covered the gaping mouth area, which she got a good look at as it turned their way. It looked big enough to be able to eat a person in one bite. The terrifying thing took a few steps in their direction.

She clutched at Raff. He rubbed her back and used his other hand to tap something else into the controls. A soft sound came from inside the shuttle and she tensed, watching as the beast outside seemed to hear it too. Its head lifted, three slitted black eyes seeming to lock directly on them, but then another sound came. It was a whoosh sound. Something shot out of the shuttle and flew past the beast.

"You missed it."

"Wait for it."

Seconds later a boom sounded in the distance. The beast spun around, running away. It could move fast and the ground shook from the weight of the thing, almost like a mini earthquake. She watched it go and the ground stopped shaking. "What did you do?" She faced him.

"It hunts by sound. I gave it something loud to go after. I shot a blast into some rock far away. Pieces of it will keep falling for a few minutes. That should keep it busy."

"That thing was huge."

"It's why outlanders need to live in caves where it's impossible for most beasts to climb."

"Outlanders?"

"People who chose to live outside of the cities." He rolled his neck and shoulders. "How do you feel? We still have a few hours left to wait. Are you hungry?"

"I could use some water to drink."

"You didn't answer my first question."

"A little tender."

He frowned. "Did I hurt you? I tried to be gentle."

"You were. It's been a while and um, you're big down there. I'm not hurt so much as you know, tender. Like I said."

He leaned over, reaching for something along the floor, and pulled out a small box. She sat back to put space between them. It was a little embarrassing now that she was more awake to realize they were both naked, she was straddling his lap, and they hadn't exactly cleaned up after sex last night. She felt wet down there and didn't want to think about how his seat would need to be cleaned.

He opened the box and removed a tube, dropped the box on the floor, and twisted it open. "Scoot back more."

She watched him spread clear jelly like substance on his finger, generously applying it. "What's that?"

He put the cap back on the tube and tossed it to back in the box, dropping that to the floor. "It will heal you." He slid his hand between their bodies and she gasped when he rubbed it between the lips of her sex and then his finger pushed inside her.

"Warn a girl! Geez!" She didn't fight though because whatever had coated his finger with felt cool to the touch and instantly seemed to take

81

away the slight pain. He had a thick finger though and he pushed inside her deep. "This is so embarrassing."

He chuckled, withdrawing his finger. "No, it's not. You're mine. I'm yours. There's nothing we can't say or do to each other that should cause that emotion." He reached down again, found a rag of some sort he must have stored down there, and wiped the rest of the jelly stuff off. He tossed the rag.

"I wouldn't quite say that."

"You should."

She glanced around the dim shuttle. "We should probably clean up and um, put on clothes."

"I'll teach you how to use the nozzle. I need to drain my bladder too."

Her cheeks heated. "Wow. You really aren't shy at all, are you?"

"No." He gripped her hips and began to lift her off his lap. "Stand to the side."

She got off him, using her arms to cover her breasts to stand in the narrow area where the door was located. He'd torn open the shirt she wore last night and completely removed it when he'd turned them over to sleep, refusing to allow any clothing to stay on her. She watched as he reached back, opened the panel he'd pointed out before, and opened it.

It shocked her when she saw the device. It looked like a mix between a large cup and a narrow, curved bowl with a white tube connected to it. It completely covered his crotch area as he lifted up a little, fitting it over his cock. He flipped the switch on the handle and she heard a slight noise like a vacuum. She averted her gaze. He was peeing. She refused to watch.

82

Raff chuckled. "You amuse me, Lilly. It's a body function. You're bright red in the face."

"It's a private body function."

"There's no privacy in a shuttle this size and we're bonded. What did I tell you? There's no need for embarrassment between us about anything." He finished, the device shutting off.

To her humiliation, he held it in one hand and tapped her thigh with his other. "Spread a little."

She shut her eyes and kept her head averted but did as he demanded. She opened her legs. He pushed the device right up against her pussy and she gasped when he turned it on. It kind of suctioned onto her and warm water hit her from her ass where the cup rose to, all the way to just over her mound.

"Release your bladder," he demanded.

"Okay." She had to concentrate to pee standing up. It was the weirdest thing ever, uncomfortable because Raff was holding the device and she didn't have to look at him to know he was watching. She had to admit she felt better though once she was done peeing. She'd needed to go. "Done."

The water cut off the flow and warm air blasted her. She tensed but then he turned off the thing and pulled it away. She felt clean down there for sure since water had blasted her. And she wasn't wet since it had also dried her off. She dared to open her eyes then and watched as Raff replaced it inside the panel and washed his hands with a steam of water that flowed inside the panel. It also blew warm air to dry them.

He closed the panel and smiled at her. "We should get more sleep." He reached for her, pulled her across his lap, and flipped the switch that caused the seat to revert into a bed. She once again ended up laying on top of him. He adjusted her until she was comfortable, her head on his chest and his arms loosely wrapped around her.

"Sleep, Lilly."

"We really need to talk about this forever thing."

"There's nothing to talk about." He lifted his head and placed a kiss on top of her head. "You're mine. I'm yours. We're bonded."

"It's not that simple, Raff." She was beginning to get worked up. He couldn't just marry her like that. They didn't even know each other. "Just because we had sex, awesome sex, doesn't mean we should be stuck together for life."

He chuckled, holding her tighter. "You could be pregnant with my child."

That had her gasping and her eyes going wide. *What? Was that even possible? No! It couldn't be.* She tensed.

"I'm not as Tryleskian as I appear. My cousin can only breed a litter with his human when he's in heat. I had the medical android run a bunch of tests on me when I first moved onto *The Vorge*. My seed is strong and viable. It's not just to prevent catching a disease that made me use a barrier over my shaft when I visited brothels. I didn't want to risk impregnating a female by accident." He kissed her head again. "With you I did it with purpose."

She didn't know if she should slap him, yell, or just freak the hell out. He was admitting to trying to knock her up. Blatantly. She sat up, straddling him. "You son of a bitch."

"My mother was quite pleasant in personality." A gleam of amusement sparked in his golden eyes. He kept one arm around her but his other one, he placed on her stomach. "My child could be inside you. Perhaps even a litter of them. I'm not certain how many I will create. We'll discover that together, Lilly."

"Litter?" Her mind worked. She had a friend once that had a dog. It had gotten pregnant and had four puppies. Is that what he meant? She was about to hyperventilate from the shock and the outrage. Hell, the panic of maybe being pregnant with alien babies. Plural. "We can't do that. I don't even know you!"

"We know each other well." He grinned, as his hand on her belly slipped lower, brushing his knuckles lightly over her clit.

She jerked at the sudden pleasure and wiggled away, trying to slap at his hand. He had fast reflexes though and dodged the contact. He gripped her wrist. He moved, rolling them until she was pinned under him. She struggled but he was big and strong.

"Damn it, Raff."

He peered at her and then went for her mouth. She tried to bite him and he laughed harder. He avoided her lips, nuzzling his mouth against her neck instead. He began to place kisses there, using his tongue and teeth. The feel of his fangs had her stilling. He could hurt her. She almost wished it did as he kept kissing her. Her nipples beaded instead and her body started to respond.

"Traitor."

He froze. "I'd never betray you, Lilly."

"Not you. My body," she grumbled.

He chuckled. "It knows it belongs to me. As mine knows it's yours." He began kissing her throat again, giving her little nips with his fangs.

It felt good. The sexy alien knew exactly how to touch her. He released her wrists, his hands exploring her breasts instead. He gave her nipples little pinches between his thumbs and fingers, making her jolt with pleasure. He applied just the right amount of pleasure and pain to have her aching between her legs.

She spread them wider, allowing him to settle his lower body between them. His cock was hard and trapped between them. He lowered down her, trailing kisses over her collarbone and then he released her breasts with his hands, using his hot mouth instead to suck on each nipple.

"Fuck," she muttered.

He growled in response. She ran her fingers over his arms and shoulders, finally ending up cradling his head. He was too good at touching her, knowing exactly how to make thinking impossible. It was all desire and need. Aliens, at least this one, made her forget everything but him.

She writhed under him, wrapping her legs around his hips. He rose up when she was whimpering, almost begging him to fuck her. He stared into her eyes as he worked his thick, hard length inside her body. The soreness was gone and there was only pleasure. He rocked his hips, driving deeper inside her.

There was a bump at the top of his cock, what felt like a ridge. It vibrated right against her clit. She cried out, digging her fingernails into his shoulders she clutched. He was like one of those sex toys she'd bought, only way better. His chest rubbed against her breasts as he pinned her tight under him, restricting her movements.

His strength turned her on more. He fucked her harder. The vibrations increased with every stroke of his hips, her clit swelling and the need to come building.

She cried out his name when the pleasure crested and exploded. She clung to him, reveling in the ecstasy he gave her. He pressed his mouth against her shoulder, muffling the sounds he made, and she could feel warm heat filling her.

The vibrations against her clit made her almost scream from how strong they had become but she had to take it since he refused to let her buck away. Another climax hit and she lost the ability to think at all.

* * * * *

Raff woke to a soft beep. He opened his eyes and realized he was mostly sprawled on top of Lilly. He'd fallen asleep after they'd had sex. Panic hit as he pushed up, terrified he'd suffocated her. She was too small to sleep under him. Her chest rose and fell though, her eyes closed in sleep. He felt relief. Another beep drew his attention again.

He turned his head, spotting it was the comms. He crawled down the bed, careful not to wake Lilly, and adjusted the volume. He stared outside. The sun had risen and there were no signs of life out there.

"Raff here."

"It's about time," Marrow snapped. "I've been pinging you for five minutes."

"I was sleeping." He turned his head, smiling as he watched Lilly turn on her side, curling up into a tight ball. She had the cutest ass and he could see it now. He also liked that it was his seed that gave her sex slit that glistening appearance.

"Well, wake up. I'm coming to get you."

"We both are," Dovis growled. "We've been monitoring the area you're in. There's four shuttles doing search patterns. I'm guessing they will attack when we come down to get you."

He leaned forward, peering out of the window. In the distance he caught view of a shuttle low to the surface. "Fuck."

"You must have been your normally charming self," Marrow chuckled. "Looks like you pissed them off badly by snatching that human I heard about. There's two more shuttles to the east of your cave. That makes six in all searching for you. You never do anything without making a lot of enemies, do you?"

"I'm no longer in the cave." He admitted. "They dropped bombs on the mountain."

"I thought no one knew about your cave." Dovis sounded pissed.

"Long story." Raff didn't want to tell them he hadn't realized they'd penetrated his hull with a tracker. "I can fly up and land in the back if you open up for me."

Marrow began to curse loudly.

"No way," Dovis snarled. "You'll damage us. You're not that good at flying, Raff. You fuck up even by a foot and both shuttles will be damaged if you slam into the side of the hold. We'll probably also be under fire. We're not dropping our shields. You'll get us all killed. Leave the shuttle. Where are you? We'll swoop in and pick you both up. We'll do a Cregion maneuver."

He hated to lose his shuttle but his gaze went to Lilly. His female was the most important thing. She must be exhausted since she still slept over their conversation. "Fine." He tapped a message to *The Vorge*, giving their location. "Time?"

It took seconds for Marrow to answer. "Four minutes. I'll dive in fast, hover, and you run for it. I take it you're shielded since I'm reading only rock there."

"Yes."

"Four minutes," Marrow muttered. "From now. We're undocked. Mark."

"Mark," he muttered, touching his arm band, setting the timer.

He twisted to where he'd left his pants, putting them on fast. He shoved on his boots next but didn't bother with a shirt. He grabbed it though, reached back, and snagged Lilly by her ankle. He dragged her closer.

"Wake up!"

His harsh, loud tone did the trick. She jerked awake and sat up, looking confused.

He released her and tossed the shirt at her. "Put it on. The shuttle is going to be here in minutes."

He pushed the button to convert the bed back into a chair and stood to the side, having to crouch in the confined space next to the door. Once he opened it, the shuttle would register on sensors. He stared out the front of window, spotting that damn shuttle in the distance still. He really wanted to kill Prix for not giving up the search.

Lilly gasped and he fought back a grin when she saw her struggling to put on a shirt while being effectively dumped into the seat the bed had become. He grabbed his bag from the storage area, shoved as many of his things he could into it, and checked the timer on his wrist. The shuttle should be in view. He peered out the front, up at the sky. A dark mass showed, barreling toward them.

He grinned then. Marrow was a damn good pilot and he remembered the time they'd been under siege on Cregion planet. Marrow had hurled the shuttle at the surface, making everyone on the ground think it was about to crash and explode.

She hadn't slowed the speed until she'd almost done exactly that. Cathian had screamed at her while they'd made their escape that the bottom of the shuttle probably had skid marks on it from the ground.

"Stand," he ordered Lilly.

She fastened the shirt front together and did it. She had to press up tight against him to find room in the cramped space.

"This is going to happen fast. Just don't fight me."

Her mouth opened.

"Trust me." He grabbed his goggles he kept in a panel section of the console, putting them over his eyes.

She looked scared but gave him a nod. "What's going to happen?"

"Better you don't know."

He shouldered his travel bag, glanced outside, and saw the hulking shape of the shuttle still coming right at them. Marrow was probably listening to a lot of alarms screaming at her with impending collision warnings.

He wanted to laugh. Dovis would be snarling and cursing. The male had no sense of humor. They'd probably have to replace the seat Dovis sat in from his claws digging into the material.

He grabbed Lilly around the waist, drawing her closer, and hit the door release. It opened, blowing hot air inside. The scent tickled his nose. He stepped out, straightened, and hauled Lilly out. It was easy to lift her and he threw her over his shoulder. She gasped but then grabbed at the waist of his pants. He saw the other shuttle in the distance begin to come closer and the sound of engines grew louder from above. He looked up, spotting his crew hurtling toward him.

"Close your eyes," he yelled at Lilly. "And hold your breath!"

The roar of engines grew louder. He couldn't hear if she responded, just hoping she listened. He probably should have wrapped cloth over her head but there hadn't been time.

The thrusters came on hard as the shuttle nose swerved up, the ground violently shaking and dirt flying. Hell broke loose as the shuttle almost slammed into the surface a good forty feet away. He held his breath and ran for the side of the shuttle that came to a sudden stop a few feet above the ground. It was hard to see with all the debris filling the air but Marrow had done this before. The doorway that opened suddenly lit up bright lights to help him see it through the dust.

He ran, holding on tight to his precious female over his shoulder, and jumped. He landed inside the cargo hold. He still couldn't breathe since dust came in with them. He glanced around, saw straps lining the wall opposite him, and lunged forward to grab hold.

The door behind them closed and the shuttle surged upward. It made his body feel even heavier with the gravitation pull of the speed in which the thrusters shot them upward into the sky. With the weight of Lilly and the bag, it almost collapsed his knees. He braced against the wall and clung to his female and the straps. The dust settled and he sucked in a sharp breath of air, panting.

The shuttle suddenly surged forward and he adjusted Lilly, allowing his shoulder to take most of the impact as he slammed into the wall. The straps cut into his fingers but he ignored the pain. The engines were loud in the cargo hold but he heard blasts. They were under attack.

A scream came from Lilly. He was glad to hear it. It meant she hadn't tried to breathe through the dust and suffocated. He released the back of her legs and fisted the shirt she wore, dragging her down the front of his body.

She almost fell but he caught her, holding her tight to his front. She wrapped her arms around his middle. He turned more, shoving his back to the wall, and got a better hold on the straps.

"Hang on," he yelled. "We'll break free of orbit soon."

He stared at the cargo hold door, debating on trying to reach it with Lilly or waiting until they were in space first. More blaster fire sounded and he just held her tighter, clinging to the straps. It was best if they stayed put until the battle was over. The shields on the shuttle could take it and Dovis would be firing back, taking out the other shuttles.

The shuttle began to violently shake and Lilly nearly collapsed to her knees. He got a better hold on her, lifted her a little, and worried with her bare feet it probably hurt her to feel that without the protection of shoes. His feet hurt in boots. They were breaking orbit. Even if their pursuers followed, if Dovis missed hitting them, *The Vorge* wouldn't. York wou d be blowing up anything chasing their shuttle.

The sound of the engines softened, telling them they'd reached space.

"It's okay," he told Lilly. "We're safe now."

She lifted her head as he eased her back onto her feet. Her features seemed unusually pale. "You people are crazy!"

He nodded. "They got us, didn't they?"

She was trembling.

That killed his amusement. "It's fine now. We'll be on *The Vorge* in minutes."

"I thought that shuttle was going to crash when I saw it and then all that dust!"

She really seemed upset.

"It's the Cregion maneuver. Marrow flies full speed at the surface but then uses the thrusters at the last second to avoid hitting it. They opened the shields just where the cargo door is to let us run in and then blast off the surface as fast as possible."

She released him and stumbled back, swaying on her feet. "I think I'm going to be sick." She lifted her hand over her mouth and made a small gagging sound.

He released the straps, shrugged off his bag, and lunged for her just as her knees gave way. He lifted her into his arms and strode toward the door, it opening when sensing him, and entered the passenger area of the shuttle. Marrow and Dovis sat in the front seats, both turning toward them.

The Vorge showed beyond them as they flew toward it. He spotted a blast of light shoot from it. York was firing on whoever who had been stupid enough to follow them into space. He flashed his two crewmates in the front a grin but turned, entering the bathroom. He made it to the sink, twisted Lilly in his arms, and she puked into the basin.

He kept hold of her, using his free hand to pull all her black hair out of the way. "It's fine, Lilly."

She retched again and he figured she had to be his mate since it didn't gross him out. Mostly, he worried about her. She finished and he released her hair, reached up to tap a panel, and it opened. He got her a mouth cleaner kit and set it down.

"Do you know how to use that?"

"Yes."

He had to strain to hear her voice. "I need to talk to my crew." He gently released her, making sure she could stand on her own. Her knees held her upright. He backed off. "I'll be back in a minute."

He watched her for long seconds. Her hands shook as she opened the kit, removing a toothbrush from the clear bag. He turned, opened the door, and exited the bathroom.

Dovis stood right there, waiting. "Is the human injured?"

"No. Just not used to space travel."

Marrow huffed from the front. "That wasn't space travel. That was me committing every pilot's worst nightmare on purpose to save my crew. Again. If I'd been off by four feet, we wouldn't be here. Our asses would be dead."

"Thank you." Raff hated to feel indebted to anyone but his crew had come to his rescue. He had gotten Lilly safely off G4.

"We have the medical android prepared to assess the human you rescued and our humans will be waiting for us to land in cargo hold one to meet her." Dovis kept glancing at the door. "How traumatized is that female? I didn't get a good look at her when you rushed from the cargo hold."

"Her name is Lilly and she's going to be fine."

Raff turned to enter the bathroom to check on Lilly but Dovis snagged his arm. He released him instantly. Raff didn't like to be touched and they all knew it. He faced Dovis.

"I need a rundown on what that female has suffered. Cathian has made her my responsibility and she's under my care. You said you rescued her from a brothel? Was she sexually assaulted? Will she feel comforted by the sight of other human females or is she mentally unstable? I won't risk her attacking Mari because she believes everyone wants to do her harm."

95

Hot rage filled him. "Lilly is *mine*." His hands instantly reached for his daggers.

Dovis's dark eyes flared wide and he took a step back. "Easy, Raff."

"Mine," he repeated. "Lilly is fine. No one will be caring for her but me. Anyone tries to take her and I'll kill them."

Dovis searched his eyes, watching him. "Understood."

"We're entering the cargo hold." Marrow cleared her throat. "Should I signal for them to clear a path or let them stay to greet us? Nobody would hurt this Lilly, Raff. You know that. Cool your temper and release the blades. We're your crew. Nobody thought you'd get attached to a female. We're just all surprised. No one meant to offend you or piss you off. Captain figured someone should be assigned to care for the human. Now you've set us straight. She's yours."

Raff turned his head, looking at her. Marrow was busy connecting to *The Vorge,* not sparing him a glance. "Clear a path."

She gave a sharp nod. "Please take her to see the medical android though. I doubt whoever had her gave her all the immunizations she needs. Gluttren Four isn't a civilized world."

"Agreed."

The shuttle engines were shut down and Marrow stood, finally meeting his gaze. She appeared stunned. "You and a human. I'm surprised. I'm glad for you, Raff." She darted a look toward the bathroom. "Does she know she's yours?"

"Yes."

"Scary." Marrow motioned to Dovis. "Let's go out there first and tell everyone to get lost. Although I'm sure they already know since the Pods are with them."

Raff watched them exit the shuttle. He turned, opened the bathroom door, and found Lilly washing her face. She didn't seem to know how to dry it though so he approached her, opening another panel, and passing her a towel.

"Thank you." She refused to look at him. "Sorry I puked."

Her cheeks were pink again. He hid a smile. A lot embarrassed his little human. "Gravitation forces that we just endured can be rough on anyone not used to it. Come. I'm taking you to see the medical android and then we'll go to my quarters. I'm sure you're hungry."

"I still feel a little sick." She finally peered up at him. "I'm only in a shirt. I can't walk through your ship."

"No one will see us until later." He focused on the Pods, ordering the mind reader race to make certain the crew avoided them for a bit. "Come, Lilly. Can you walk or do you want me to carry you?"

"I can walk." She straightened her shoulders.

He felt proud of her. She was a brave female, for having such a frail body. He held out his hand, offering it. "Come."

She took it. He grinned, knowing she was his.

Chapter Seven

Lilly felt nervous as Raff helped her sit on a medical bed and the robot approached her. Raff went to back away but she clutched at his arm to make him remain close. They didn't have anything like the android on Earth. It had the shape of a humanoid form, only all metal, and she noticed the four fingers and two thumbs on each hand.

"It's safe," Raff urged.

"Hello, human. I'm the medical robot." It had a cold, sterile male voice. "What may I do for you today?"

"Total scan and blood tests," Raff ordered. "She's from a planet that never went into space until recently. Pirates stole her. Check to see if she was given any vaccines and fix that if she's missing any."

"Right away. Please lay flat," the android instructed.

Raff met her gaze. "It's all going to be painless. I'm right here."

"Okay. Please keep close."

"Always."

She released him and lay on her back. Lights flashed over her body, a stream of blue starting at her feet. It didn't hurt. Something tapped the back of her leg but it was very light and didn't hurt. A holographic imagine startled her more when it hovered over her. She stared at it, her mouth hanging open. It was her but on the inside. She could see her organs, bones, and every other part of her under her skin.

"It won't take long," Raff encouraged. "You're doing fine."

She darted her gaze to the android. He moved to a wall and scans lit it up. Dozens of screens flashed. Data streamed across each one but she couldn't read what they said since it was too far away and not English. Something cold touched her shoulder blade and then there was tiny prick. She gasped, jerking.

"Hold still, please," the android ordered, not moving away from the wall.

Raff took her hand. "Blood and tissue samples are being taken. It's fine. You won't have a mark on you when this is done."

The technology was incredible. If anything, she could appreciate that. They'd had a real medical staff on *Bax*, even if it were just two people. She glanced up, regretting it. The hologram above her was zooming in on various parts of her body, including her lungs. She could make them out, including every vein in them, looking away fast. It made her feel sick.

Raff crouched down, his grip on her tightening. "What's wrong? You're breathing hard."

"I don't like getting exams and seeing my insides. We have skin for a reason."

He grinned.

An alarm beeped and the android spun, coming at her.

"What's wrong?"

"Nothing to worry about," its cold voice stated.

Raff stood, released her, and allowed the android access to her. "Report now."

"Kapintor cells have been found inside her body. I'm eradicating them."

"What?" She felt panic.

"Easy," Raff ordered. "It's curable. You probably came into contact with it from the Rexis."

It was easy for him to say. Part of the bed side slid open and a panel slid out. The fingers on the android tapped on it and something jabbed her in the ass. She gasped, wanting to roll way. Raff was there in an instant, holding her still. He leaned in. Another alarm beeped.

"Easy, Lilly.

"You are confusing the scanner with your body, crewmember Raff," the android instructed. "Move away."

"Trust me," Raff rasped. "Hold still."

She gave a sharp nod and he backed off. The alarm stopped and she got another jab, that time to the back of the thigh. She closed her eyes. Something wet rolled down the back of her naked calf. She grimaced but didn't flinch away. It felt as if the table licked her with a wet plastic tongue. It ended.

Minutes passed but nothing else happened. The hologram over her shut off and the android backed away. It faced Raff.

"Two immunizations were missing. The Kapintor cells are destroyed. Her lungs showed slight damage. It's been fixed. Would you like a full report?"

"Send it to my cabin. I'll study it later. Is she healthy?"

"Now she is."

"Thank you." Raff helped her sit up and lifted her off the table. "Let's go. I'm sure you're ready to eat. I sent a mental comm to the Pods to ask Midgel to deliver food for us."

"The what and who?"

He led her toward the door. "Pods are another alien race. Three of them live on the ship. They have strong telepathic abilities. They are able to hear you if you think at them. Midgel is the cook."

She nodded. "Telepathic? Mind readers? I read about a race that could do that but they were the Valer something or other."

"Later once you've eaten and rested, I'll introduce you to the rest of the crew."

Another thought struck and she quickly stared up at him. "You can't read my mind, can you?"

"I wish," he muttered.

She kept staring at the ship as they moved through corridors and even took a lift to another floor. It was a nice place, way better than *Bax*. The walls weren't just metal sheets and beams. It reminded her more of a fancy hotel. Raff finally stopped in front of a door and it opened. She gawked a little. Speaking of, it was a nice suite she stepped inside.

"This is our cabin," he rasped.

She turned to face him. "We still haven't talked about this um, marriage thing. Our cabin? I didn't say I'd live with you."

He stalked to her, wrapped an arm around her waist, and cupped her face with his hand. "There's nothing to talk about."

"The android thing would have said if I were pregnant, right? That means no shotgun wedding is needed."

He scowled. "Shotgun wedding?"

She put her hands on his firm, warm chest. He wasn't wearing a shirt and that distracted her. The guy had an amazing body. "Never mind about that. The android would have told us if I were carrying a baby or babies, right?"

He caressed her cheek. "You're not pregnant."

She felt relief, having enough on her plate to deal with at the moment without that too.

He smiled. "Yet. We'll fix that."

"Raff!" She pushed against his chest and tried to jerk away. He let her go. She put space between them, walking to a couch, and taking a seat. He was assertive and confusing. She lifted her hands, burying her face in them. The urge to cry or maybe scream hit. She wasn't sure which one was stronger.

Something creaked near her and she looked up as Raff shifted his weight where he'd taken a seat on the coffee table in front of her, or what passed for the alien version of one. He grabbed hold of her hands.

"Talk to me. What have I done to upset you?"

"Nothing. Everything. You confuse me so much. Half of me wants to agree to this craziness but the other part knows it can't end well." She held onto his hands rather than rejecting the comfort he offered. He'd been the only good thing to happen to her since the aliens had attacked and taken her from her work vessel. "It's all so crazy, you know?"

He nodded.

"Leaving Earth was to be an adventure but it wasn't supposed to be forever."

"Why did you want an adventure?"

She hesitated but decided to unload on him. "I grew up in a remote desert area in a place called Nevada. The nearest large city was a few hundred miles away. Not that we ever went there. My parents and grandparents ran a solar power farm. Sometimes they'd hire extra workers if there was storm damage, too much for us to handle on our own, but mostly, it was just the five of us all year round."

He listened, watching her, but didn't say anything. It encouraged her to continue.

"They didn't want me to go away to college, too worried something bad would happen to me. I had to argue with them to do it and we compromised. They found a school in a smaller city in Arizona. There were only a few thousand students. I was really excited to go but once I got there, I realized I didn't fit in."

"Were the students not human?"

"Oh, they were all human. I just had zero in common with them. My social skills were bad, as you can imagine. I focused on my studies. I dated a few guys but it turned into disasters."

His features turned harsh. "They hurt you?"

"I was stupid and naïve." She let go of his hands and ran them over the shirt covering her thighs. "I came from a family where you fall in love, get married, and stay together forever. My grandparents celebrated fifty-

103

three years of marriage before I left Earth. My parents were married for twenty-seven years. Let's just say that when a guy told me he loved me, I saw us having kids together and the whole nine yards."

"Nine yards?"

"It means everything. Anyway, while I was mentally planning our wedding, he was plotting his next conquest. I learned he was never serious about me. He tossed that L word around to get girls in bed with him and once he got bored, he'd look for a new girl."

Raff frowned.

"Then I met another guy, we dated, and he said he loved me. He even asked me to marry him. I said yes and took him to meet my family. It turns out he figured us owning a solar farm meant we had to be extremely rich. He dumped me when he found out that wasn't the case. Solar farming is hard work, it earns a decent living, but never enough to become wealthy. I grew smarter and stopped trusting men. I got hit on a lot but most of them did that to every woman. Like it was a game to see how many they could get into their beds. I wanted no part of that."

"They were idiots."

"Thanks. I appreciate you saying that." She smiled. "Then I graduated college and landed a great paying job at a large corporation. I was stuck in this small cubicle, staring at walls. Day in and out. I lived in a large city finally but I understood why my family hated them once I did. Nobody talked to me and making friends was impossible. Everyone is too busy and I wasn't exactly outgoing. I'm actually quite shy."

He frowned.

"I am. Don't look so surprised. You met me while I was trying to avoid being raped. Shy doesn't mean I won't fight to protect myself. Back to what I was saying, I spent four years at that job and I saw my future there if I stayed. Lonely, horrible, and boring. That's when I overheard two of the women I work with talking about a job that was opening up. It was *Bax.*"

"The ship you were stolen from?"

"Right. I worked for the company that launched it. Those women in the breakroom were going to apply for the data entry job and gossiping about how many hot, single men would be there. They had heard that all of them would be single and how the last time a mission went out, seven couples hooked up and got married."

Raff looked confused.

"I saw my opportunity. You know, that maybe I'd meet someone and they'd fall in love with me. For real. Worst case, it wouldn't happen but I'd get to go into space, see cool stuff, and have a great story to tell. I wouldn't be staring at a wall every day. Only I got there and the guys just wanted casual relationships."

"What's that?"

"They didn't want anything serious. It was like a game again. You know? Just having sex to have sex and nobody wanted to enter real relationships. I wanted no part of that and once again, I didn't fit in. The men were rude to me after I turned them down."

"They don't sound like good males."

"Tell me. The real reason I left the farm was to meet a guy. Do you know what it was like watching my parents and grandparents be together while I was always alone? I wanted to have what they did. Someone to love and be happy with for the rest of my life. I never met anyone my age or even close to it on the farm. All the seasonal workers were always way older or already married."

"You met me."

She smiled. "I did. You're the best thing about all this, Raff." Then she felt sadness. "But we don't know each other well enough to be married yet or have babies. It also means I have to pick between an uncertain future with you or trying to find a way to get back to my family. You said Earth is a banned planet. It hurts thinking I won't ever be able to see them again." Tears filled her eyes.

He moved from the table to sit on the couch next to her and just scooped her up into his arms, setting her on his lap. "Two things, Lilly."

She sniffed, wiping at her tears. "What?"

"Our future isn't uncertain. I am not like the humans you've known. I want forever with you and children. There will be no other females. No games. I don't play them. Everything about me is serious."

She could believe that about him.

"Also, there is no way to return to Earth. I've told you why. I can promise you though that you can send communications to your family. There's no ban on that and if there ever is, I'll break the law for you. You can see your family through comms."

She turned into him and wrapped her arms around his neck. It broke her heart to hear him say she'd never get to hug her parents and grandparents again. That's what it boiled down to. Sobs hit her but he held her.

"I'm sorry," he whispered against her hair. "We'll send them comms as much as you wish. You won't lose your family."

Raff felt guilt when he ignored the door chime. It had to be Midgel with their food. Consoling Lilly was more important. She finally cried all her tears and he carried her into the bathroom to take a shower. He promised her food when she was done. He crossed his cabin, opened the door, and went to pick up the covered meals. That wasn't all that waited outside the door.

Cathian looked up at him from where he sat in the hallway, legs stretched out, ankles crossed, and a data pad in hand. "It's about time. I thought I'd be out here for hours." He reached up and tapped his ear. "One said your female is upset and why."

Raff stepped out into the hallway and let the door close behind him. "Don't," he threatened.

Cathian frowned. "I haven't said anything."

"You'll want to find a way to get a transport to return Lilly to Earth. They are selling their females. She will remain safe with me."

"I wouldn't do that. The Pods read you before you even stepped foot on *The Vorge* and warned it would be a bloodbath if any of us tried to get between you and that female. We weren't waiting for you outside the cargo hold. The area was cleared to give you and Lilly privacy." Cathian set down the pad and climbed to his feet. "Do you really think I'd try to take away someone who matters so much to you?"

"You wouldn't if you're smart."

A grin spread across Cathian's face. "I'm happy you found a female. Shocked." His humor died. "But relieved too. Three said the female is torn between wanting to be with you and trying to return to her family."

Raff nodded. There was no reason to deny it.

Cathian reached inside his pant pocket and held out an ear piece. Raff scowled at it, not moving to take it.

"One is on the other end of this. Do you want help or not?"

"What is he going to do?"

"Read your female's thoughts, help you say the right words to her, and get her to agree to life-lock to you. I asked the medical android to save the scans it took of her for the medical procedure. It can be done at any time."

Raff took a step back. "There will be no procedure done."

Cathian opened his mouth, looking furious, but he paused. "What do you mean he isn't able to give her his second heart?"

Raff moved fast, tearing the small device from his cousin's ear, and threw it on the floor. He yelled in his head. *Stop reading my thoughts and sharing them with Cathian, damn you. You never want to piss me off.*

Cathian scowled at him. "Was that necessary? The Pods are trying to help and from the look on your face, you just threatened them."

Raff growled low.

"We all want you to keep your human."

Raff believed that. "I'll win her on my own."

108

"Fine. Explain to me why you won't life-lock to her then. That will prove to her that you're serious about your intentions to keep her forever. She has doubts about that."

"I'm not you."

"God damn it, Raff." Cathian looked angry again. "I get it that you had a bad childhood, but you can't bring a human onboard to just have sex with. The Pods said you're serious about this Lilly and have deep feelings. That means life-locking to her."

Raff moved fast, pinning his cousin against the wall. "I can't because I don't have a second heart."

Surprise etched across his cousin's face. Raff released him, spun away, and put a few feet between them. He didn't want to see the lock in Cathian's eyes. "I have some of my mother's traits," he confessed.

"I didn't know."

"I didn't tell you."

"Tell me now."

Raff turned, prepared to see pity. His cousin showed none. Just curiosity.

"I don't have a second heart and I've never gone into heat."

Cathian's mouth opened but he said nothing.

"My seed is always fertile. I had the android run tests on me when I first came onboard and ordered it to erase the results when we were done. Your family hates me enough without discovering that I'm flawed."

"I don't give a damn what the Vellars think or feel." Cathian stepped closer and raised his hand, gripping his shoulder. "You are not flawed in any way. Never say that again."

Raff gave a sharp nod but it made him feel relief that his cousin wasn't repulsed.

"Do you want to keep Lilly? Bond to her?"

"Yes."

"What do you need to do to make that happen?"

"I don't think there is a physical way to lock us together," he admitted. "People on G4 just decide to live together and breed. Once children come, they tend to stay together."

"What did your mother tell you?"

"That one day I'd feed off a compatible female and it would trigger my heat cycles to begin. I fed off at least half a dozen different females. When that didn't happen, she said they weren't a match. It was denial on her part. She was able to feed a Tryleskian and couldn't have been the only one on the damn planet compatible to my father."

Cathian nodded. "Agreed. Have you fed from Lilly?"

"Yes."

"Nothing?"

He smiled. "I wouldn't call giving her pleasure or how good she tastes nothing."

A chuckle escaped Cathian. "True. I feast on Nara all the time and I'm no longer in heat."

"The android said I should be able to get a human pregnant. I don't care about going into heat. My seed is fertile all the time."

"Do you know if you'll have litters?"

Raff shrugged. "I would like to have young with Lilly. I don't care if it's one or more at a time."

"Good answer." Cathian released him. "York had a ceremony with Sara. I'll sit the crew down and we'll come up with something special for the two of you. I am an ambassador and captain of a ship. It gives me certain powers. I've also had to inform our home world of life-locked males with alien females before who live on other planets. I'll do that with you and Lilly to make it official. The Vellars never need to know you don't have a second heart."

"That's breaking a rule."

"Fuck the rules."

Raff grinned. "Do it. I wish I could see the faces of our fathers when they learn I have a female. It's going to upset them greatly."

"I'll record the live comms when I tell them. You can have a copy of it. When do you want this ceremony?"

Raff thought about it. "I'll let the Pods know. I need more time to convince Lilly."

"I have faith in you."

Chapter Eight

Lilly couldn't help but smile. Raff was going out of his way to be a total sweetheart. She'd taken a shower and when she'd come out, he had a meal set up for them on the bed. He'd excused himself to get clean, before joining her. They'd eaten and he'd shared nice stories about him and his mother.

It made her ache for him when he told of how his mother had been murdered. The pain in his voice had made her reach out to touch him. He'd even had tears in his eyes.

"They were criminals I went after," he admitted. "I didn't care when they were just stealing from people but then they decided to get into the meat business. They kidnapped some of the city residents to take to the outlands to use as bait."

That confused her. "Bait?"

"You saw a fasis."

As if she could ever forget their early morning huge visitor outside the shuttle. She nodded.

"There are a lot of large creatures that size in the outlands. Selling their meat to the cities is very profitable. The best bait to lure them into a trap is something alive and bleeding. Especially if it makes noises like screaming."

"I get it." It sickened her. "How could anyone do that to someone else?"

"That's why I was hunting their group down. To put a stop to it. Instead they heard I was tracking them and attempted to kill me first. My mother paid the price. I wasn't there to protect her. I'll always live with that guilt."

"You had no way to know what they'd do, Raff." She hesitated and then crawled across the bed to snuggle up against him. "You were trying to save people."

He put his arm around her and rested his chin on her head. "It was a dark time for me after I found her body. Then my cousin came seeking me. I thought he was an assassin sent by my blood father to kill me."

She gasped, peering up at him. "Why would your father do that?"

"He's a dick. I'm a huge embarrassment to him. It would be easier for him if I were dead and it's not the first time he sent someone to kill me. When I was a child, my mother contacted that family trying to get me off world. G4 was dangerous. Tryleskians came but they were assassins. That cave I took you to? My mother and I lived there for a few years until we figured it was safe to return to the city."

"Not a dick. An asshole!" She felt anger for Raff.

"He never meant for my mother to get pregnant and he has no honor since he abandoned us. Cathian found out about me when he took the job as ambassador. His father warned him in case my mother made another claim or I did. My cousin was ordered to destroy any comms about my claimed association to the family. Instead, it enraged Cathian. He tracked me down, apologized, and swore to stand with me against them. Then he offered me a new life at his side. That's how I came to live on *The Vorge*."

"Your cousin sounds pretty great."

"Cathian is a male with honor. I trust him with my life."

"I can't wait to meet him." She meant it.

"You'll like everyone on this ship and they'll feel the same way about you."

"I've never been good at making friends, remember?"

"You've never met ones like us. We're all…" he seemed to be struggling to find the right words.

"Special?"

He chuckled. "Yes. That's better than what I was going to say."

"What was that?"

"Flawed with qualities others don't appreciate. We're a loyal group. A family. It's the first time I've had someone to watch my back without expecting it to come with conditions or a price. I trust them with my life and yours."

"Mine?"

He stared down at her. "Yes. You're one of us now that we're together."

She studied his eyes. He appeared sincere. "Just like that, huh?"

"Just like that." He smiled. "They want to hold a bonding ceremony for us when you're ready."

He shocked her. Was he talking about a wedding?

"We could record it and send it to your family. That way they will get to see us join our lives together in an official capacity. I know it's not the same as being there themselves but it's as close as possible."

She teared up. Raff had a way of doing that to her. It was considerate that he'd think of her family. "Married?"

"Same thing. Different word. Forever."

"I..." She was tempted to say yes.

"What are your fears? That I'll change my mind and later regret making a lifelong commitment to you? It won't happen. Tryleskians bond for life. My mother's people do as well. My mom never took another lover after my father. I wish she had but she said they'd bonded. No other male could draw her attention. I read about humans." He scrunched up his nose and looked disgusted. "We do not *divorce*."

He almost made her laugh. "You said that like it's a nasty curse word."

"It is." He suddenly lifted her and shifted on the bed, falling back with her on top of him. The dishes from their meal rattled as the mattress moved. "I should be more worried about you, little human."

"Me?"

"Yes. Your world has that word. What's to say you won't want to leave me?" He ran his hands along her body until he cupped her ass with his hands. "I will have to show you often how good of a husband I will be and how no other male will ever give you what I can."

She bit her lip, realizing he had a point. Divorce rates where she came from had risen to eighty-four percent. Out of their two races, it sounded like hers was the bad bet. "You forgot about my parents and grandparents. Lifers."

He smiled and rolled them, pinning her loosely under him. "I like that term. Lifers. We shall be lifers, Lilly."

He was so handsome and she couldn't resist reaching up to touch him. "You make it sound so easy."

He peered deeply into her eyes. "I'm bad at talking but you are the one thing that is easy for me. Feeling for you and wanting to keep you. I've felt protective and wanted you since the moment I saw you running from the Rexis and coming toward me. Every moment I've spent with you since makes me want even more time with you. It's never going to be enough. How do I make you feel?"

"You've been amazing at talking, actually."

He smiled. "You're the only one who will ever say that. Trust me."

"Really?"

He nodded. "I normally say few words. It would shock my crew if they could hear us speak."

She liked that a lot.

"Answer my question. How do I make you feel?"

"So many wonderful things," she confessed. "Inside my head I keep telling myself we're too different though. But then you touch me or even look at me, and I don't care. The thought of leaving you, even if I could return to Earth, makes me hurt because I know I'd miss you. Badly."

"You're never going to find out for certain. I'm right here and will remain so. Stop thinking, Lilly. I've survived by listening to my instincts. Tell me how you feel."

He wanted her to be honest. She understood that. "I'm falling in love with you, if I haven't already."

His grin was large and showed off those sharp fangs of his. They no longer scared her. They were sexy. She knew exactly how good they felt when he lightly raked them over her skin.

"We're meant to be together, Lilly. My mother believed in fate, despite what the male she bonded with did to her. She said he gave her a son and that I was everything to her. I was on G4 right where I needed to be when you arrived and you ran to me. You fell right at my feet when you were shot with that stunner."

"Did I?" She smiled. "I was kind of distracted with the whole trying to avoid those bad guys."

"You did. I instantly wanted to kill to keep you safe. Instinct, Lilly."

"Maybe you're just a really good guy."

His expression turned somber. "I'm not. For you I am and always will be. Others should fear me. Only you bring out the best in me."

She wanted to believe that. It sounded romantic.

"Stay with me, Lilly. Life can be difficult but us being together is not. We'll always have each other."

Something her grandfather had told her many times suddenly surfaced in her memory. It was how difficult it had been starting the solar farm and expanding it. Her family had never become rich but he'd swore that no matter what difficulties he'd faced, one kiss from her grandmother had made it all melt away. Even after all the years they'd been together.

Raff was right. She needed to stop overthinking everything. Her grandmother would urge her to take a leap of faith. That's what she'd done when she'd married a man who dreamed of harnessing the power of the sun.

"Yes."

He leaned in closer, his lips almost brushing hers. "Yes to a bonding ceremony and accepting me?"

She nodded. "I'm scared, I have no idea how this is going to turn out, but yes."

He kissed her and she closed her eyes, loving the way he made her feel. Sexy, desirable, and extremely turned on. He shifted his body over hers, pushing at the shirt she wore. She wiggled, helping him get her out of it. He backed off and ran his golden gaze down her body.

"You're mine, Lilly. I *will* get you pregnant. We'll have as many young as you wish."

He wanted kids. It was important to her. Raff was right for her. He might be an alien, this might not be the life she'd envisioned growing up, but it didn't matter. Only he did.

She sat up and reached for the waist of his pants, opening them. A low, sexy growl came from him. Raff was a super hot alien Viking cat man and all hers. He helped her shove the material down and she stared at his cock. He was not quite human there but the shape was the same. Only he was thicker and way better. She knew that from experience.

He took her flat to the bed, his mouth going for her breast. She felt him kick something and the dishes from their meal hit the floor as he scooted down a bit. She laughed.

118

Raff lifted his head, chuckling. "I'll clean that mess later."

"I don't care," she confessed, sliding her fingers into his hair and tugging him toward her breast again. "Just keep touching and kissing me."

"Demanding. I like it." His mouth closed over her nipple and she moaned his name.

Raff was right. Being with him was easy. It was thinking that screwed her up. There was no sense in worrying about the 'what ifs'. It was more about focusing on the 'here and now'. That was a philosophy she could adapt and live with.

* * * * *

Raff loved the taste of his human. Lilly's skin was as sweet as her personality. The nipple he teased grew taut as he released it with his mouth and softly blew his breath across the tip. The scent of her arousal teased his nose as he ran his hand down her soft belly to between her legs. She spread her legs for him and he traced the seam of her sex, finding her wet. The sounds she made excited him more. His Lilly enjoyed his touch.

He slid lower, pushed her thighs farther apart, and began to feed from her. He might not need female hormones the way his Tryleskian brethren did but she gave him a high. It was almost like dr nking Cathian's expensive booze he broke out during important meetings. Only Lilly tasted better.

Her fingers dug into his hair and he almost grinned. She had small hands, dull little finger claws, and he loved the way she scratched at his scalp. It felt good. Everything about her did. The little bud at the top of her slit swelled and he sucked on it, her moans growing louder.

It amused him the way she always tried to press her thighs together right before she came. He held them open and growled, knowing she loved the vibrations. That did it. His Lilly cried out his name and pulled his hair. He eased his mouth off her little bud and lowered his mouth, licking her slit. He couldn't get enough of her taste.

He lifted off her and climbed higher up her body. Lilly's head was thrown back and she released his hair to run her hands down the sides of his arms. Her eyes were closed, her mouth parted a little as she tried to catch her breath. He grinned, gripped his shaft, and lined their bodies up. He pushed into her, released himself, and used his arms to brace most of his upper weight off hers. It was a concern to not crush his small female. She had to weigh half of what he did.

Her eyes opened and she moaned as he sheathed his shaft inside her tight, hot body. He loved the way she felt. Her hands slid up and she gripped his shoulders. Her legs lifted, hugged his waist, and wrapped around him.

He began to thrust his hips, grinding them against her, as he watched her face. She was beautiful to him in passion. He adjusted his hips, learning what she enjoyed best. The sounds she made helped him figure that out. Soon her pussy clamped tight around his shaft and she threw her head back, his name on her lips. He followed in an explosion of ecstasy, giving her his seed.

He rolled off her, taking her with him, to avoid crushing her smaller body. She felt right in his arms. He couldn't help but grin.

Pods, prepare that ceremony for in the morning. Something a human would like. Ask Nara, Mari, and Sara for advice.

He'd double check later that they'd picked up his thoughts. Lilly would become his forever.

Chapter Nine

Lilly was nervous as Raff positioned her on the empty bridge in what she was certain was the captain's chair. He walked over to one of the consoles to the side, bent, and went to work. Her gaze locked with the huge viewing screen. After she talked to her family, Raff was taking her to breakfast to meet the crew.

"I'll step out when we connect to give you privacy."

It was thoughtful of him. She was worried about how her family would react over seeing an alien. "Will you stick close? I'd like them to meet you once I tell them everything."

"I'll keep the door open. Turn and wave to me when you're ready. I'll be back far enough to not overhear your conversation. I respect that you want privacy for this."

"Thank you for this, Raff. Tell your cousin I appreciate it too." Raff had gotten permission from Cathian for her to make the super long distance call. He'd even cleared the bridge.

The screen went from showing outer space to a bright room and a gray-haired woman wearing glasses squinted into the camera. "Hello?" She glanced away. "Honey, this darn thing is acting up again. It was ringing and I answered but it's all static."

"I'm boosting the signal," Raff whispered.

Her grandmother's eyes widened. "Lilly?"

"Hi, Grandma." She grinned and lifted her hand, giving her a wave.

Her grandfather was suddenly behind his wife, peering at her. Tears filled his eyes. "Lillian." His voice broke but then he cleared it. "We were told you died."

"I'm alive." She fought back her own tears. "How are you guys? How are my parents?"

Her grandfather turned his head. "Ray! Dana! Get in here. It's Lilly! She's alive!"

Her grandparents stared at her and then her parents crowded in behind them. Her mom burst into sobs and her father clung to her. "Baby, it's you. They said the ship blew up and all souls aboard were lost."

"It's a long story but I'm fine. I'm going to send you some condensed files. They are letters I wrote you this morning to tell you everything." She felt tears slipping down her face and reached up to wipe them away. "I'm in deep space and the signal won't last long. I just wanted you to know I'm okay and I met someone. His name is Raff and he's amazing. I think you'd love him. He saved my life."

"Are you on your way home?" Her mother got control of her sobs, sniffing.

Lilly felt her chest tighten. "No. Read what I wrote and you'll understand. I'll keep sending you letters and I'm getting married. Expect a vid. I wish you could be here but I'm happy." She stared at her grandmother. "I took a leap of faith, Grams." Her gaze fixed on her grandfather. "Raff's kisses make everything better, Gramos." Finally, she looked at her parents. It hurt her to see them so upset. "I love you guys so much. It's going to be fine. I promise." She turned in her seat and saw Raff standing in the hallway, watching her from just outside the door.

123

She held out her hand toward him. He came to her fast, walked right to her side, and crouched down, staring at the screen. Lilly looked at her family, seeing their expressions when they got a look at her Viking cat alien man.

"This is Raff. He actually saved my life a few times. He's everything I've ever been looking for and I love him."

"I swear I'll die before I allow anything to happen to Lilly. She's my heart."

Raff's words made her grin wide.

"You're an alien," her father whispered. He didn't look unhappy, just stunned.

"I'm a Tryleskian, sir. An honorable one. I also sent you a letter to introduce myself to your family and references. I have a good job and can provide well for your daughter. She'll be safe with me."

Lilly gasped, looking at him. "You did?"

He smiled at her. "Your family is important to you. That makes them important to me."

"He's handsome," Grams whispered. "Looks tall too."

"He looks like he can protect her," Gramps murmured. "Look at those muscles on him. He's a big fella."

"She always did like cats," her mom whispered.

Her father cleared his throat. "When are you returning to Earth? We want to see you both."

Raff stood, staring at the screen. "I'd love to bring Lilly there but it's too dangerous. Your Earth isn't telling you everything. They are selling your women to be slaves to aliens."

That had all four of her family wide eyed and paling.

Raff continued. "They've also attacked some colonies on other planets. She's safer with me. Read the letters."

The screen got fuzzy, static lines running through it. Lilly stood. "I love you!"

She saw her family's mouths move but the sound didn't come through. She put her hand to her lips and blew them a kiss. Her grandfather lifted his hand, opened it, and pretended to catch it. The comms cut and space showed on the screen once more.

Raff put his arm around her. "I knew it wouldn't last long. I'm sorry."

"It was long enough. Thank you so much." She turned into him, wrapping her arms around his waist and buried her face against his chest. "They thought I was dead. Now they won't have to grieve my loss."

He rubbed her back and pressed a kiss on her forehead. "I sent the letters with the transmission. They reached your family with the live feed. We'll comm them again soon."

"I'm okay. It was just so hard to see them but I'm grateful."

"They looked like nice humans."

She laughed. Raff had a way of doing that when she was feeling down.

"We could meet the crew later if you wish."

She shook her head. "I want to meet them now." She eased away enough to peer up at her alien. "I'd like the distraction."

He leaned down to brush his mouth of hers. "I'm proud of you."

"Why?"

"I know that was difficult but you did it."

"I'm not going to overthink anything. Let's go meet your cousin and everyone else."

He kept an arm around her as they left the bridge and walked to the lift, entering it. They got off on another floor and he led her to the dining room. The doors opened and she took in the faces of Raff's crew family.

Some of them were very odd but he'd prepared her for the Pods. It wasn't every day she got to see aliens who resembled egg people. One big guy with a lot of muscles was blue. The other alien male looked a bit scary, even in skin, and Raff had warned her that sometimes he was a lot furrier since he was a shapeshifter. Part of her was excited to see both sides of him. Her attention turned to the women.

It was nice to see three humans after so many aliens on the planet. It made her feel less out of place. One of them jumped up and came at them quickly. She knew it had to be Nara since she'd been sitting on the lap of a man who resembled Raff.

"Another human! Welcome to *The Vorge.* Give me a hug."

Raff let her go and she was almost tackled in a bear hug. She squeezed Nara back. Two more humans approached her. Raff had described the women's looks, as well as things he knew about them. Mari gave her a smile and a wave. Sara hugged her too.

126

The remaining two females hung back. The cook was a tiny alien and extremely anti-social. The taller woman with fuzzy fur skin regarded her with a stern expression but it wasn't unfriendly. These were Raff's crew and the people she'd live with.

Lilly was really looking forward to getting to know them. She was just a little worried since making friends wasn't really easy for her to do. It was important to Raff that she fit in though.

One of the rounded Pods stepped closer and smiled at her. "You'll fit in here fine, Lilly. Relax and just be yourself."

The tension eased from her body and she smiled back at him. "Okay. Thank you."

"Now, the questions," Nara chuckled. "Prepare to play twenty questions. We want to know everything there is to know about you."

* * * * *

Raff watched everyone interact with Lilly as they stood in the dining hall. He could tell she was slightly uncomfortable but she didn't freeze up. The crew asked her to tell them where on Earth she'd come from and a little about how she'd ended up in space. She'd handled the questions easily and didn't seem offended.

He kept close, ready to come to her aid if that changed. His crew could be nosey. Pride tightened his chest though at how she bravely conversed, despite her fears of not making friends.

"I can't believe you have a mate." Marrow stared at him, before focusing her attention on Lilly. "Everyone wants to know if Raff talks to you or just grunts and growls."

Lilly turned to their pilot and smiled. "He talks my ear off and never shuts up."

The entire room turned quiet, all gazes fixing on him. Raff shrugged. "I like to talk to Lilly."

Cathian shot him an amused gaze. "And other things."

"*Many* other things," he agreed.

York opened his arms as he came forward but then rethought hugging him when Raff met his gaze.

York stepped back, dropping his arms. "This is great. I'm happy for you, Raff. Who knew you had a heart to give to a female? It's a nice surprise."

Raff narrowed his gaze at the male and touched the blade strapped to his thigh. York took another step back. Raff suddenly chuckled. "Lilly *is* my heart."

York smiled. "You need to work on that sense of humor still. I thought you were going to stab me."

"He wouldn't do that." Lilly pressed up against his side.

York lifted his sleeve to show off a faint scar. "He would. This was a warning for when I tried to get him to sing with me. I was glad he didn't go for any vital organs."

Lilly turned her head, peering up at him.

Raff shrugged. "It was just a warning that he had become annoying. He tried to put his arm around my shoulders. I don't like anyone touching me."

"You like it when I do." Lilly winked at him. "I can live with you getting stabby if other people put their hands on you though. Especially if it's a woman. I'm the jealous type."

"I am too."

"Shit," Nara whispered. "Imagine what is going to happen if we take her to a bar with us while we're visiting somewhere. Raff is going to slaughter every male in the place that stares at her too hard."

Dovis growled. "He'll have help if they look at my Mari too."

"Yes, he will," York agreed. "We have to protect our beautiful mates."

Cathian just laughed. "I guess we'll hold all of our celebrations on *The Vorge* from now on. It will be much safer for other races that way."

"Speaking of, we should eat and then start getting ready for the ceremony." Mari smiled at Lilly. "We had a wedding dress made for you. I hope you don't mind but I got your measurements from when you sought medical treatment from the android. We wanted to make sure it would fit."

Lilly looked surprised and her mouth opened but no words came out.

Raff spoke for her. "Thank you." He glanced around at his crew. "We appreciate you putting a marriage ceremony together for us on short notice."

"Thanks," Lilly whispered.

"It's our pleasure." Nara took a seat on Cathian's lap again. "We're so happy that you two are together."

"She might make him less bloodthirsty," Midgel muttered.

Raff glanced at the cook and she darted into the kitchen. Lilly tugged on his hand and he met her gaze. Her eyebrow arched in question.

"She was joking."

"No, she wasn't," Marrow stated. "We're all hoping now that Raff has a female he'll mellow out. We're glad you're here, Lilly. It's hell cleaning up bodies all the time or fixing the messes his body counts cause."

Raff glanced at her.

Marrow shrugged. "It's the truth. You do like to kill people. I bet you didn't leave that planet without taking someone out. You never do."

He wished he could deny it to look better in front of Lilly but he wasn't a liar. "Fair enough."

Lilly stood up. "He did kill people but they were the assholes who stole me off my ship and then tried to make me become a prostitute. I think you're all being unfair. He didn't kill anyone who didn't deserve it. I'm here because of him saving me. I might not have known Raff as long as you all have but he's an amazingly sweet and thoughtful man. Caring and wonderful. You're making him sound like some psychopath who kills people for the fun of it. That's not true!"

He grinned, happy that she'd stood up for him, and grabbed her around her waist, pulling her onto his lap as he took a seat. "That's my female. Fiercely defending me."

"You must be *really* good in bed," Marrow muttered under her breath.

He shot her a warning look. He didn't think she spoke loud enough for the humans to hear. The last thing he needed was for Lilly to question her choice to bond to him. Marrow gave him a slight nod, sealing her lips.

Midgel returned from the kitchen, carrying plates. "Breakfast is ready."

He kept Lilly in place when she tried to scoot off him to eat. "I like you here."

She smiled at him. "It seems to be a family trait." She glanced at his cousin and Nara.

"Must be a Tryleskian trait to have our females on our laps." He lowered his voice, putting his lips close to her ear. "So is feeding. I wish you were spread out on this table for me to feast from."

Lilly blushed and he chuckled. His little human did embarrass easily.

"I'm so happy," York stated loudly. "Look at us. Our family is growing." He glanced at Sara. "Tell them."

Sara glanced around at everyone and a grin spread across her face. "We're pregnant!"

Most of the crew broke out in cheers, getting up to hug the couple. Raff remained in his chair holding Lilly but he felt a little envy. He wanted to have a child with his female. They would. He was determined. He caught York's eye and smiled at him to show he was pleased for the mated pair.

Marrow hugged them but then he noticed that she slipped out of the dining hall. He understood. It was tough to see so many couples when one was alone. He'd been there. Lilly had saved him from that though. He held her a little tighter. She was his heart.

Chapter Ten

Raff worr ed as he waited on the bridge for Lilly to be brought to him. She'd left their cabin with the other females an hour before to prepare for the ceremony. It was a human custom to not see the bride before the couple were married.

"Stop fondling that knife you strapped to your thigh," Cathian ordered. "You look like you're ready to go kill something, despite only wearing one weapon instead of dozens. They will be here soon."

"What if she changes her mind?" Raff felt lucky that Lilly agreed in the first place to bond to him. He did tend to scare everyone, especially females.

"She won't." Dovis drew his attention. "You saved her life and you're different with her. Softer. Females appreciate that."

"She's on her way here now," Two stated.

"She loves you," One told him. "Very much."

Raff glanced at Three, waiting for him to weigh in.

He did. "She's fearful that you'll change your mind."

"Never." Raff's gaze locked on the doors to the bridge.

"This is unbelievable," Marrow snarled.

Everyone looked at her.

She shrugged. "Raff gets a mate before I do? This is so fucked up." She held his gaze. "No offense."

"None taken. I'm surprised too. I never saw this coming but I knew the moment I saw Lilly that she was mine." Raff ran his hand down the front of his uniform that he rarely wore. "Pure instinct."

"It must be," Midgel added. "I don't know why anyone takes a mate otherwise."

The doors slid open and he watched as Mari walked in first, followed by Sara, and finally his Lilly was being escorted by Nara. That was another human tradition. A family member usually walked the bride to where the groom waited. He lost the ability to take a breath as he stared at his female.

Lilly always looked beautiful to him but they'd done something different with her black hair. Some of it was piled in twists on top of her head, while curled long locks trailed down her shoulders. The white dress molded to her figure, accenting every curve. Her smile was radiant. Moisture flooded his eyes and he had to rapidly blink to clear his vision. He couldn't believe she was really his. She was too good, too sweet for him. Not that he'd ever give her up.

"Get over here so I can claim you," he growled.

She laughed and tugged out of Nara's hold, rushing forward. He moved to meet her, gripping her hips. They stared into each other's eyes. He just wanted to throw her over his shoulder and return them to their cabin to strip her bare.

Cathian loudly cleared his throat. "Soon. I don't need to be one of the Pods to know what you're thinking. Face me. I'll make this fast."

Raff took a deep breath and nodded, tearing his gaze from Lilly. He slid his arm around her though, refusing to stop touching her. The crew members had all put on their official uniforms for the wedding. Cathian even donned his ambassador sash.

"It is an honor for me to bring this couple together today." Cathian smiled at both of them. "Raff, do you take Lilly to be your mate, your wife, and bond to her in all ways until the end of time?"

"I do." He stared down at her as he gave her his vow. "I dare anyone to ever try to take her from me."

"We all know that. Death and destruction will rain on any bastard who tries." Cathian chuckled. "Lilly, do you take Raff to be your mate, your husband, and to bond to him in all ways until the end of time?"

She nodded. "Yes, I do."

"At this time, couples usually exchange wedding rings but that's an Earth custom and you aren't bonding to one." Cathian paused and turned, then took a small package from York. He turned back. "Lilly, Raff has given you full body armor."

York laughed. "To make sure nothing ever happens to you."

Raff shot them dirty looks. "It's romantic."

Lilly took the package. "It's so light!" She grinned up at him. "You bought me body armor? I love it. Thank you."

He grinned and reached into his pocket, withdrawing a small gold band. He lowered to his knees in front of her. "That's not all. Give me your left hand."

She held it out and clutched the package to her chest. He noticed she slightly trembled. He took her hand in his and slipped the ring onto her correct finger. He'd asked Nara for advice beforehand when he'd had it replicated. He stared up to her. "I want to give you everything."

Tears slipped down her cheeks. "You have. You do."

He rose to his feet and narrowed his gaze on Cathian. "Now."

His cousin nodded. "With all my authority, I bond the two of you in marriage and decree you are life-locked. You may claim your female."

Raff scooped her up and spun, striding out of the room with her cradled in his arms. "Thank you!"

Lilly wrapped her arms around his neck and he felt the package in her hand against his back. "Where are we going?"

"You heard him. I'm going to claim you. That will be in our cabin. No one will dare interrupt us until tomorrow."

"No kiss, huh?" She had a teasing tone.

"There will be lots of kissing but not in front of everyone else. That would mean we'd have to stop once we start. Not happening."

She laughed. "I totally agree."

He increased his pace, wanting to get her to their cabin faster. The plans he had included a waiting special meal for them to share and a few more gifts. Lilly needed a lot more clothes and he'd asked the other females to replicate a few dozen outfits. They were waiting for Lilly to unwrap. Females loved presents. He was going to make certain Lilly never regretted choosing him.

* * * * *

Marrow entered the shuttle and sealed the doors. It was her place to escape from the crew and had its own long-range comms system. It would be embarrassing if she were caught talking to prospective mates in Cathian's office or on the bridge.

"Raff found a mate. Raff." She still couldn't believe it. He was the least friendly male she'd ever met. She'd never even considered climbing into his bed. His personality gave her nightmares. Until she'd seen him soften for the human, she was pretty sure he only got aroused by killing or touching his precious weapons. "Raff." She shook her head.

She reached up and finger combed her hair, turning on comms. Messages waited and she began to read the profile of the first prospective mate who thought they'd be a good match. Her lips curled back in disgust at the alien who'd applied. He was a parasite. Literally. His needs stated that he'd latch onto a female's body to ride their backs through life.

"Not a chance."

She went to the next message and read it. This one sounded interesting until she got to his image. She winced. He had two heads, eight eyes, and stood three feet tall. She deleted that one.

Depression hit. Most of the males who were looking for females were sad creatures. It would have been funny if she wasn't serious about finding a mate. She had standards though. Attraction was at the top of her list, along with someone who was at least her size or larger. The race didn't matter.

The next message killed her interest fast. He was looking for multiple females to bond and breed children with. She guessed he hadn't read her profile before sending his. It happened often too.

"Stupid male. I won't share." She deleted him.

The next one had her lean forward. He was a Tryleskian. She smiled. They were larger than her, into only one female, and she didn't mind a little surgery to life-lock to one. His career was listed as a supplier of trade goods and that he traveled often. He was looking for a female who didn't mind living on a ship. That was her! Excitement built. She clicked on his image and gasped. It was a face she knew.

Anger came next. The information she'd read was a lie. Jorgan Reek had stolen that image and must be trying to run a scam. He wasn't her captain's littermate brother. She tapped on the contact information, ready to threaten him with death. The screen in front of her came on and she placed the connect. It wasn't immediately answered but then a face came on.

Her mouth fell open. "Cavas? It's really you?"

He smiled. "It's about time. Don't you check your matches, Marrow? How are you going to find a mate if you ignore males who reach out to you?"

"Jorgan Reek?"

His expression grew somber and he leaned in, lowering his voice. "It's a false identity I'm using right now. Cathian mentioned you were hunting for a mate. I logged onto the system in hopes of finding you."

She was stunned. Her and Cavas didn't get along. He was in the military and had a very controlling personality. She'd left her home world to avoid males like him. "You want to mate me?" She curled her lip to show her displeasure at that idea.

He chuckled. "No. We'd be a terrible match."

"I know. That's why you're confusing me right now."

He glanced to the side for a second, then met her gaze. "I'm going to intercept *The Vorge* in about six hours if you don't change course. I left this message for you yesterday. You really should check them more often. I've been worried you wouldn't respond in time."

"You're making no sense, Cavas."

He reached up and ran his fingers through his short hair. "I'm going to dock with *The Vorge* but I need you to shut down some of the systems to prevent any record of it."

"You are confusing me more."

He closed his eyes, sighed, and then opened them. "I'm trusting you. My father gave me orders I refused to follow. Then Crath went missing in retaliation. I do what our father has demanded or I have a feeling we might never see my youngest brother again."

Marrow gasped, stunned. "But Crath is his son. You, Cathian, and Crath are from the same first litter your mother birthed for him. That makes the three of you special and important in your family."

"Never think Beltsen Vellar won't sacrifice family. Ask Raff."

Dread pit in her gut. "What was the order?"

Cavas hesitated.

"You said you trust me. Tell me what your father ordered you to do."

His golden eyes flashed rage. "Kill Raff after I obtain some documentation he has against our family."

Marrow tensed. "I'm not letting you kill Raff. He has proof that your father hired assassins to come after him and his mother when he was a boy."

The rage on his face increased and he snarled. "One more betrayal."

"I won't allow you to harm Raff. He's family."

"I would *never* do that. That's why Father did something to our youngest littermate. I refused! I need Cathian's help to find Crath or we may never get him back."

"We all will help." Marrow gave a sharp nod.

Cavas's features relaxed. "Don't tell my brother about this. I need to talk to him in person or he'll confront Father. Cathian has no idea how dangerous he's become. I do. We need to find Crath first. I'm in a shielded shuttle but I can't dock with *The Vorge* without your assistance. I am certain my father is monitoring your ship's main computer. I need you to take some systems offline to prevent it from registering my arrival and that I'm onboard."

She bit her lip. "I can do that."

"That's the easy part. I need another favor from you."

"What's that?"

He hesitated. "I left my personal shuttle docked at Rave Station. It will be monitored by our father too."

She frowned, confused again.

"When I dock, I want you to take the shuttle I'm in, fly to Rave Station to pick it up, and then use it to go traveling far from *The Vorge*.

They'll think it's me. Pack your bags, Marrow. You're about to get a vacation."

Her mouth fell open but she recovered. "I can't do that. I'm needed here. Some of the crew can fly a shuttle but not as well as I can."

"You forget that I was trained as a shuttle pilot and am probably better than you are. Look at it this way, Marrow. I'm taking your job for a while until we find Crath and instead of looking at profiles, you can actually meet males. You're not going to find a mate on comms. Look at the kind of shaft heads who contact you." He grinned, pointing at his own chest. Then laughed.

She growled. "Fine. I'll pack."

"Don't forget to shut down those systems I need you to and prepare for me to dock with you in six hours."

"Captain is going to be angry," she predicted. "I better have a job and a shuttle to come back to."

"As if my brother would ever lose one of his crew for good. Your job is secure. He's just getting a bonus one once this is over."

She frowned again.

"Me, Marrow. I resigned from the military when my father asked me to kill my own cousin." Anger flashed in his golden eyes again. "There's going to be one more Tryleskian added to your crew." He winked. "See you soon."

She stared at the dark screen when he cut comms and sighed. She wasn't sure anyone on *The Vorge* would be happy when they learned

Cavas was about to join them. She stood, shutting down comms and left the shuttle. She had systems to turn off and a bag to pack.

Up next…Cavas

About the Author

NY Times and USA Today Bestselling Author

I'm a full-time wife, mother, and author. I've been lucky enough to have spent over two decades with the love of my life and look forward to many, many more years with Mr. Laurann. I'm addicted to iced coffee, the occasional candy bar (or two), and trying to get at least five hours of sleep at night.

I love to write all kinds of stories. I think the best part about writing is the fact that real life is always uncertain, always tossing things at us that we have no control over, but when writing you can make sure there's always a happy ending. I love that about being an author. My favorite part is when I sit down at my computer desk, put on my headphones to listen to loud music to block out everything around me, so I can create worlds in front of me.

For the most up to date information, please visit my website. www.LaurannDohner.com

www.ingramcontent.com/pod-product-compliance
Lightning Source LLC
Chambersburg PA
CBHW020401130626
46549CB00006B/2392